GHOST FISH

"A refreshingly playful take on magic realism, *Ghost Fish* turns the idea of a grief novel on its head. With wry humor and real feeling, this wise new writer shows the lengths we'll go to in order to cling to those we love. A pitch-perfect portrayal of the chaos and heartbreak of sisterhood."

—Marie-Helene Bertino, author of *Beautyland*

"Alison is twenty-three and alone in the world. One night she is visited by a ghost in the shape of a fish that bears an uncanny yet unmistakable resemblance to her dead sister. Thus begins Alison's deeply moving, often hilarious—and ultimately life-affirming—journey to confront her grief while also figuring out how to rejoin the land of the living. Stuart Pennebaker's debut is full of tenderness and deep feeling. I loved it."

—Laura van den Berg, author of *State of Paradise*

"*Ghost Fish* is a luminous novel of grief, sisterhood, and the necessary magic we need to bridge loss and healing. Stuart Pennebaker has written a shimmering, otherworldly exploration of love that persists beyond the boundaries of life and death. A dazzling, original debut that will leave you forever changed."

—Chelsea Bieker, author of *Madwoman* and *Godshot*

"For all those wistful fresh-eyed girls trying to find their way in that Big Rotten Apple, Pennebaker has written the anthem! *Ghost Fish* demands your utmost empathy as we follow Alison in the City of Dreams, a newbie restaurant hostess and lonely heart navigating sketchy dates and striving for reinvention, all while her reincarnated sister-fish shakes her fin! I devoured this book in a weekend. It is spooky, heartfelt, tender, and, above all, never afraid to go there."

—Sidik Fofana, author of *Stories from the Tenants Downstairs*

"An otherworldly exploration of siblinghood, grief, and loneliness, *Ghost Fish* reminds us that there is nothing stranger—or more human—than loss. This book will hang around like a specter long after you've put it down."

—C. Michelle Lindley, author of *The Nude*

"A gorgeous, heartfelt story about a floundering girl trying to start over and the loss that won't let her go. Brimming with hope and yearning, along with a sly dose of absurd charm, *Ghost Fish* manifests a truly original haunting to lead us gently and lovingly through Alison's grief." —Kerry Cullen, author of *House of Beth*

GHOST FISH

A Novel

STUART PENNEBAKER

LITTLE, BROWN AND COMPANY

New York   Boston   London

Copyright © 2025 by Stuart Pennebaker

Little, Brown and Company
Hachette Book Group
1290 Avenue of the Americas, New York, NY 10104
littlebrown.com

First Edition: August 2025

Little, Brown and Company is a division of Hachette Book Group, Inc. The Little, Brown name and logo are trademarks of Hachette Book Group, Inc.

The publisher is not responsible for websites (or their content) that are not owned by the publisher.

The Hachette Speakers Bureau provides a wide range of authors for speaking events. To find out more, go to hachettespeakersbureau.com or email hachettespeakers@hbgusa.com.

Little, Brown and Company books may be purchased in bulk for business, educational, or promotional use. For information, please contact your local bookseller or the Hachette Book Group Special Markets Department at special.markets@hbgusa.com.

"Poem ('Light clarity avocado salad in the morning')" on page 124 from *The Collected Poems of Frank O'Hara* by Frank O'Hara, copyright © 1971 by Maureen Granville-Smith, Administratrix of the Estate of Frank O'Hara, copyright renewed 1999 by Maureen O'Hara Granville-Smith and Donald Allen. Used by permission of Alfred A. Knopf, an imprint of the Knopf Doubleday Publishing Group, a division of Penguin Random House LLC. All rights reserved.

Book interior design by Marie Mundaca

ISBN 9780316587631
LCCN 2025930858

Printing 1, 2025

LSC-C

Printed in the United States of America

For Mills

PART ONE

IT WAS A TUESDAY NIGHT, but the air vibrated like it was a Friday. I wondered if all of summer would be like this. Full of potential. I stopped at the bodega on the corner for a veggie sandwich. It tasted like French fry grease and I felt like something rare and precious, eating a bodega sandwich while I walked down a city street. When I was halfway to Jen's apartment, I realized I had nothing to drink, and I wasn't sure if her invitation was for me to drink her drinks at her apartment or if I was supposed to bring my own. I turned back and bought three single cans of Tecate at the bodega, then opened one on the sidewalk and had that as I retraced my steps.

A few weeks before, I'd turned twenty-three and realized I could hold every good memory I had in one hand. I lived alone in my dead grandmother's empty house. My mom was dead; my sister too. I didn't need originality; I just needed to be alive. So I messaged a boy named Tyson on Craigslist who had space to rent in a four-bedroom in the East Village, gave my two weeks' notice, emptied my grandmother's house of all the dusty, useless things she'd left behind, and took bright bouquets of grocery-store flowers to the graveyard where everyone I'd ever loved now lived. And then I packed my car and drove away from the town that clung to me with every single tentacle of its octopus body.

Jen and I had grown up together in Awnor and still loosely referred to each other as friends. We were from the same patch of nowhere land, a negative space she'd shed four years earlier and that I'd only just escaped. She was someone who'd known me well enough to attend my mother's funeral when we were fifth-graders, and my sister's when we were old enough to truly understand what death meant. But she'd vanished from my life when she'd gone away to college. Still, she was the only living person I knew in the city, so when I'd packed my car and pointed north a few days prior, she was the only one I told. We hadn't spoken for some years, but she responded to my message with lots of exclamation points and invited me to "pre-drink drinks" at her apartment. I hadn't met my roommates yet or put sheets on my bed, and most of my clothes were still in trash bags on the floor of my tiny room, but I was eager for my new life to begin.

When I got to Jen's building, I stared at the silver box on the wall. There was a button next to her unit, 7C, but I wasn't sure if the correct etiquette was to buzz her or text her. I pressed the button, but nothing happened. Then I heard a loud metallic sound and Jen's voice, distorted and robotic, yelled through the speaker: *"Come up!"*

I opened the heavy glass door. A doorman sat at the desk.

"Good evening," he said as I entered the building. A gush of AC made the loose strands around my face blow straight down.

"Oh. Hello. I'm Alison."

"Hello, Alison." He wore a uniform that included a cap perched like a bird on top of his head. It was silent for a moment and I felt awkward, like maybe I wasn't supposed to introduce myself.

"Seven C," I said. "That's where I'm going."

"Elevators are right around the corner," he said.

I could hear the hum of a party from inside Jen's apartment when I stepped off the elevator. It sounded warm and busy. Fun—that's what it sounded like. I almost forgot I would know exactly one person at this party, or pre-drink drinks, or whatever it was. I knocked on the door.

"Alison!" Jen shrieked as I stepped inside. She was tiny, a piping plover, light brown hair streaked with expensive-looking highlights that were new since the last time I'd seen her. She threw her arms around my neck. "Oh my god, I am *so-fucking-happy* to see you. It has been so long. So, so long!" She sounded like when we were teenagers and she'd tried tequila for the first time.

"Oh my god," she said again before I'd had time to reply. "You did not have to bring beer! We have plenty of stuff. You're so cute! And tan! How was the move?"

I smiled. I had almost forgotten about Jen's boundless, relentless happiness. I'd seen her truly upset only once, sobbing in the girls' bathroom in high school after she made a D on a math test. Even that was just for a moment before she returned to herself, tied tight again in a perfect pink bow.

The first time I ever went shopping in Belk, the only department store in Awnor, was the day before my mom's funeral. My ears felt like they were full of cotton. Everything was a dull roar. But neither my sister nor I had black tights or coats, and it was January, and dead people are typically buried outside, so our grandmother took us shopping. I was in the dressing room behind a red curtain staring at my reflection in the mirror, realizing I looked nothing like my mom, when Jen poked her head through the curtain. Her face was like a pale, full moon. We were in the same homeroom, although we weren't really friends yet. She walked straight into the curtained-off room and said she'd run into my sister in the shoe section. Then she sat on the bench in the corner of the tiny room and started talking about coats and shoes, her favorite brands of clothing, did I know Trevor tried to touch Beth's boobs after the fifth-grade dance, could I believe that, and she'd never really stopped talking at me until she went away to college.

"Hi, Jen," I said. "It's good to see you."

She released me from her tight squeeze. "Let's get you something to drink!" she said, her voice bright.

I followed her through the enormous kitchen and past a flight of stairs to a large room of chatting, perfectly dressed humans.

"Mark!" Jen said. "Meet Ali!"

Mark was Jen's boyfriend. We'd never met but I'd seen photos of him on social media. He was shorter than I'd anticipated.

"Yo," he said. "How was your move?"

"Good, thanks." I shifted my weight to my other leg. "It still feels kind of surreal to be here."

"Right on," Mark replied.

"Mark, take Al to get a drink. I've got to run upstairs to check on Lauren, my roommate," she told me. "I think she did coke."

I smiled weakly at Mark's back as he pushed through the crush of bodies in the living room. I couldn't believe Jen lived in an apartment with two floors.

There was a bar cart in the corner with a silver ice bucket engraved with the words *Gramercy Hotel*. Mark put ice in a red plastic cup and said, "Gin and tonic?"

"Please," I said.

"Yo! Noah!" Mark said, looking past me. He gave someone a bro-y high five over my head as I turned to introduce myself, and I found my face pressed into a guy's chest.

"Noah, Ali," Mark said.

"You must be Jen's friend. The new girl," Noah said. He smelled like salt and damp soil or something fresh. He was much taller than me and reached down, gave me a side hug as he said hello. I flinched, then wrapped an arm around his back. My stomach flipped. I wasn't used to people touching each other as a form of hello. I realized I was still standing very close to him, and I took a step back. I wasn't sure if I liked the way he said *new girl,* but I did like the way he'd entered the room, as if we'd been waiting for him. I liked the way he smelled. I cleared my throat.

"Noah and I went to college together," Mark said. "Now we work at the same hedge fund."

"Oh," I said. "That's nice."

They both smiled in a forced way, the kind of smiles that follow a silence where words should have been.

"Is that for me?" I asked, pointing at the red cup in Mark's hand. The beer I'd chugged on the sidewalk, or maybe Noah, the strange, almost primal reaction I was having to him, had made me feel a little bold.

"Oh, shit, yeah. Sorry."

I took the cup from his hand.

"It was nice to meet you," I said to Noah. "I'm going to go find Jen. Lauren did cocaine."

"Nice to meet you, Alison," Noah said. He had half a smirk on his face. I didn't want to leave him, oddly, but didn't want to stay close either. I set off in search of Jen, the word *crush* like a Greek chorus in my head as I walked away. I hadn't had a silly crush in such a long time, the kind that was based on things like the length of a boy's eyelashes and the way he said the word *hi.* Was this what it was like? Maybe. I felt a little thrill at the potential of a crush, of being at its precipice.

Jen was in the kitchen, bent over the counter. For a second I thought she was snorting something, but when I got closer, I saw that she was cutting limes into half-moons.

"I don't actually know why I'm doing this," she said. "I didn't even know we had limes."

"Oh, okay," I replied. "Um, how are things? With you? Mark seems nice."

"He's so great." Jen's eyes looked flat. She was still cutting, wielding the knife in a surprisingly deft fashion. I watched her divide the last lime into six clean wedges. She put the knife down and looked at me like she had something important to say. She opened her mouth, then closed it again.

"Do you want to borrow something to wear?" she asked finally.

Instead of feeling offended, I nodded and followed her through the crowd in the living room, up the magical, impossible stairs, to her bedroom. It was white in a bleached-teeth way: white walls, white bed frame, a white marble desk. I felt the distinct tickle of central air on the back of my neck as I slipped off my shirt. Jen's closet had white slatted accordion doors. She opened it and pulled a blouse from a hanger. I slipped it on and, of course, it felt as if a tide pool were a piece of fabric. I was sure it cost more than my rent, but I was surprised to find that I didn't care if Jen had so much compared to my single room and anonymous roommates.

"How are you?" Jen asked. Her voice was level and serious. We hadn't had a falling-out or anything, but after my sister died, we'd drifted apart. I'd barely noticed until Jen was gone, off to college, and I realized my last text from her was months old. I was surprised she'd asked. Jen was historically not one for deep conversations.

"I miss her," I said. *Her* meant so many people.

"Of course," Jen said.

"This is beautiful," I said, gesturing to the blouse. "Thank you."

"Okay, yeah. We should probably go, right?" Jen asked. I felt both disappointed and relieved that she'd let me change the subject.

"I mean, it's only eleven, but there will be a line at Ray's." She squinted at her phone. "Yeah, let's definitely go. Mark!" she called. There was no way he could have heard her through the closed door and down the stairs, not to mention over the din of bodies pressed against each other outside her white room, humming, a low roar. But almost instantly, he opened the door.

"Ready?" he asked. We followed him through the throngs of bodies in Jen's living room and out of the building.

"How's the city so far?" Noah asked me as we stepped into the murky air. It was newly strange, summer in a city. It felt different to be so hot and so far from the wide-open ocean, although we were standing on an island, technically.

"I'm not sure yet. Today is my first full day," I said.

"Do you live around here?"

"Yeah, a few blocks away," I said. "Where do you live?" I asked. I could feel the heat of a blush licking at the tips of my ears, flushed beneath his attention. And then I felt embarrassed at the embarrassment pinking my face.

"Midtown. We city-biked here."

"Right," I said, pretending like I knew what he meant by *city-biked.* "Hey, Jen," I called out. Noah and I were walking in a pair a few yards behind Jen and Mark, who were drinking out of matching pale pink coffee cups with giant handles. Three girls who looked like models were walking a few yards behind us, and I found it very strange that nobody had introduced themselves yet. I felt like the rule was that the person who was outnumbered didn't have to initiate the introductions, but maybe I didn't know anything at all.

"What's up?" Jen tossed over her shoulder.

"Who's Ray?" I asked. She laughed and pointed toward the end of the block at a building that was painted purple with the word RAISE in a neon-lit sign above the dark-tinted doors. I had misunderstood. I was strangely disappointed to still be so close to my apartment.

We joined the back of the line. Jen leaned against a metal gate protecting a storefront.

"Oh my god," she said suddenly, startling me. "I totally forgot! Al, this is Noah. Noah, this is my friend from home I was telling you about! And she's a freaking Gemini!"

"We met," Noah said. I felt my cheeks pink all over again.

Jen smiled and shook her head, pleased, as if she could tell the future and knew something we didn't.

"I knew it," she said. "I knew you two would like each other."

When I looked up again, Noah was taking out his ID to show to a bouncer in white go-go boots and a purple shirt that matched the walls of the building.

"Coming?" Noah asked. I removed my Georgia driver's license, bendier and brighter than his piece of plastic issued by New York, from my wallet. The bouncer took what felt like hours to find the birth date.

"Bottom right," I finally said, and he nodded and handed it back to me. I ducked into a dark room that was lit by disco balls dripping from the ceilings, stacked on the bar, attached to the walls. I couldn't see Jen or her friends and stood still, scanning the room for a familiar face. I felt an arm wrap around my shoulders, and every inch of my body went *hummmm* and I was hip to hip with Noah.

"We thought we lost you," he said.

"I knew it!" Jen said again, behind him.

I danced like a fish out of water flailing its hopeful body. A tall girl named Victoria said: "Shots!" Mark said: "Does anyone have Adderall?" A Prince song played and another girl, also named Victoria, sang, "'If I came back as a dolphin, would you listen to me then?'" She had a stunning voice, raspy and clear at the same time. I wanted to be exactly like her, sexy and in my skin and so, so pretty.

It was a painted-purple club with a waterbed instead of bar stools, so of course Noah and I danced closer and closer. It was an uninspired mix of music, but we were not deterred, the breath from his lips hot against my neck until I was ready to dissolve.

"Be right back," Noah said, motioning to the bar. I nodded and backed away from the dance floor, leaned against the wood-paneled wall. I was feeling a little lightheaded and then, suddenly, very bad. Tequila-Adderall-tequila-bad. I hurtled away from the wall and toward the exit, flung open the glass door, vaulted outside, and threw up into a trash can. The air felt warm and damp, and I was empty. I could still almost feel the bass in my ears and breath on my neck, and I laughed, delirious, into the velvet night air. I pulled Jen's one-shouldered blouse away from my body with my fingertips and shook it to create a personal breeze. It looked like something a Greek goddess would wear, but black.

The line to get into the club was now wrapped around the block. I felt bold in my goddess shirt and walked to the front of the line, up to the bouncer in the shiny white go-go boots who'd checked our IDs a few hours ago.

"Hi," I said.

"No," he replied.

I shrugged. "Fine. I like your boots."

"Still no, princess. Go home."

I checked my phone. It was dead, which seemed like a sign. I walked two blocks in the wrong direction, then turned around and walked back. I found the dry cleaner's and the scaffolding with HOMESICK graffitied on it in electric-yellow paint, my new north stars. The streets were quiet. I wondered if anyone would notice that I'd left without warning, disappeared from the purple-painted club like water on a summer-hot sidewalk.

I reached out my hand, let my fingers brush the metal grate of the closed laundromat as I passed. I tried to remember the last time someone had worried about me. I couldn't.

I woke up sweaty, still wearing the blouse I'd borrowed from Jen the night before. The mattress was wedged between the room's one window and the wall, like spinach stuck between two jagged teeth. For a moment, I couldn't remember where I was. The narrow room looked alien, then came into focus: East Village. Avenue D. Apartment 2B. A room that used to be a hallway with a window onto the fire escape. My new home.

My head felt like it was full of wadded-up tissues and shards of glass, and I could smell tequila emanating from my pores. I felt my cheeks burn. I was a bit embarrassed about disappearing the night before until I thought about Noah's breath on my neck and curled my toes. I wanted to lie there all morning and watch the hot sun move across the room, but I had a job interview and I really did need a job.

In my old town, I had been the manager of a very small bookstore–slash–coffee shop. My boss's husband had grown up in New Jersey and knew a guy who knew a guy who managed a restaurant in the West Village. The guy's name was Brandon, and he'd agreed to interview me for a job at three p.m. my first Wednesday in the city—which was, unfortunately, today.

All of my clothes were still in trash bags on my floor, and every article of clothing I owned now seemed deeply uncool.

Sunlight poured in through the window yawning over my bed and my room felt unfairly hot. The heat, the smell of my grandmother's house still clinging to my clothes, all of it made my head pound. Even the plastic of the trash bags felt warm against my skin as I stuck my arms inside, scrounging around for something to wear. My instinct was black jeans and a black top but all black seemed to scream, *I just moved here! I've read too many magazines about what people wear in New York!* I tried on a skirt and a sweater, but this combination looked like something a teenager would wear to prep school. One of my roommates was talking on the phone while she heated something up in the microwave, and I wished so badly that I was the kind of person who could throw open my door and make a quick friend, ask to borrow a dress or pants or an opinion.

I was not that person. I was surrounded by bags full of items that had seemed essential back home but felt dorky and dated now. My bed didn't have sheets yet. I had three roommates and nobody to ask, *Does this make me look hot but capable?*

Try the black pants with the split hem, I imagined my sister telling me. *And that blue silky top. It looks good with your eyes.*

My sister was dead. She'd died when she was sixteen and I was seventeen. People called us Irish twins until they called us nothing at all. She drowned in the ocean under a tilted black sky and I became nothing. I couldn't help it—I still wished her back into the room, able to tell me what to wear.

I put on the blue shirt and black pants, put my wallet in a bag that had belonged to her, a sequined Coach purse she'd found at Goodwill when she was in eighth grade. It shimmered in the sun like good luck, and I crossed my fingers. My bank account, after the night before, had dipped into the low triple digits, and I still hadn't bought things like a subway card or milk.

The restaurant was a twenty-minute walk from my apartment, all the way down St. Marks until it turned into Eighth Street. I'd worked in restaurants before, always as a host. It wasn't host*ess* anymore, because of feminism, my last manager had told me. I missed the beautiful hiss of the *ess,* but I wasn't sure if that made me a bad person. My first job was at a sports bar where they called us "sauce girls." There were no feminists managing that particular institution, nor the fancy steak house where I worked during summers, the busy season in Awnor. So when a bookstore with a coffee shop opened in a strip mall near the highway, a minor miracle in our small town, I'd migrated there.

I loved that bookstore. The tips were okay, and I liked the other kids who worked there, Kate and Dillon, especially Dillon. I had an anxious, desperate crush on him. He listened to music I hadn't heard of and read books by people none of my teachers talked about, and he didn't play sports like most of the guys I went to high school with.

He had a girlfriend, of course. Her name was Lillian, and she was from two towns over. Her family lived in a house on the beach that looked like the vacation homes that were usually vacant, owned by people who mostly lived elsewhere. Her lips were a perfect bow, and the first time she came in the store to visit Dillon, my crush on him evaporated like hot milk and landed on her. She was unselfconscious, had long dark hair that was so shiny, it looked like it had another dimension. I wanted to drown in that hair like it was a spring tide, its water moving fast and deep, or rip it off and staple it to my scalp. She was sea foam collecting in every corner of my body. She was other-worldly, especially in a place so barren. It was the first time I'd had such a physical reaction to another person. I spent hours scrolling through her social media. I wanted to soak myself in her and emerge a bit closer to the kind of person she was. Ever since, desire and identity had felt confusing. I wasn't sure what I wanted more: for Lillian to put her mouth on the softest parts of my body or for Lillian to vacate her pretty life and let me have it.

My sister was still alive when I worked at the sports bar but not when I worked at the bookstore. It was strange that she didn't know about Dillon or his tulip tattoo or his beautiful girlfriend or how it felt when Kate and Dillon and his beautiful girlfriend and Jen all went off to college and I stayed at the bookstore, sold iced coffees and cheap thrillers to tourists, and lived in our grandmother's empty, dark house.

I looked at my watch. I'd walked too fast and was early for the interview, so I turned left to walk down Fifth Avenue until it ended at Washington Square Park. The park smelled like city garbage (banana peels, dead things, stale coffee), which was different from the tang of Awnor (dirt, dust, the tide changing). The fountain in the middle of the park was turned off; boys without shirts, lines of sweat pointing toward navels, zigzagged in and out of the concrete basin on their skateboards as people stood around the arch in clumps, taking photos of themselves.

I pulled my phone out of my bag and looked at my messages: nothing. Nobody had noticed that I'd left early the night before. I tried not to feel disappointed. It was probably for the best; I had a sense that Noah was a seabird and I was a washed-up fish—something he'd eventually swallow whole. I sat on a bench, my legs sweaty against the wooden slats, and rolled my shoulders back, trying to find some height, as a man with a pierced nipple skated a figure eight around me. I typed out a *Hi* to Jen, hovered my thumb over the blue button for a moment before pressing Send. A group of girls who looked a year or two younger than me, probably college students, all laughed loudly at something. I tried not to stare at them, their separate laughs all threaded into one.

My phone read 2:56. I put it back into my bag and retraced my steps back up Fifth Avenue toward twinkle lights strung from a building over an outdoor patio. A server in a crisp white oxford walked down the three marble stairs at the front of the building with plates balanced along each arm, and the patrons sat quietly, wearing expensive-looking sunglasses, with newspapers or iPads in their hands. I walked quickly past the woman at the host stand, peculiarly positioned outside, not wanting to introduce myself before I knew whether or not the job was mine. It felt like bad luck. The name on the front of the building read THE JUNE, in all capital letters. I wiped my sweaty palms on my pants and walked inside.

The restaurant was located in a hotel; it was not entirely its own entity. The lobby looked like a page ripped out of a coffee-table book, all perfectly mismatched rugs and deep couches. Armchairs were covered in velvet and the built-in bookshelves were stacked with titles like *Whitney Biennial, Yves Saint Laurent Archives*. I felt young and very new. I walked to the front desk.

"Hi," I said. "I'm here for an interview?"

The concierge had a face like a '90s model. He was all angles, sharp cheekbones, and eyes so dark they looked liquid.

"For..."

"The restaurant?"

"Dining is back through the lobby. Go left through the bar."

"Thanks so much!" I said in my best and brightest customer-service voice.

"You're welcome so much!" he replied, mocking my false tone.

The bar was old-school elegance, red vinyl booths and smoky mirrors showing cloudy reflections, and the dining room behind it was spacious and bright in comparison. A marble host stand stood sentry at the entrance, and I tried not to be intimidated that the restaurant was seemingly busy enough to require two host stands, one outside and one in. The marble one in front of me was so large that I almost didn't notice the woman about my age standing behind it, scribbling on a white pad of paper. She wore a green top with a lacy collar and reminded me of someone I knew or maybe someone famous, but I couldn't think of who.

"Hi. I'm here for an interview," I said again. "Are you the manager?"

"Aren't you adorable," the girl said, pen still to paper. There were rings on all her fingers except her thumbs. They glittered like Popsicles just pulled from a freezer. It was not a question.

"Um. Can you tell me where to find him?"

She finally stopped scribbling on her pad and looked at me as if she were appraising a car. She hadn't been writing, I realized, but doodling. An intricate vase full of flowers was scratched on the notepad in blue ink. It was actually quite pretty.

"I'll buzz Brandon," she said finally. She put down her pen and picked up the receiver of the phone on the host stand. The phone was mint green and shaped like a retro rotary phone but it had a normal keypad on it. She punched a few buttons, then hung up.

"You can sit," she said, gesturing with a hand in the direction of the dining room.

The room behind her glowed in the afternoon sun slanting

in from a skylight. Plants tendriled from the ceiling, dripping toward a floor tiled in blue and white ceramic.

"At a table," she prompted. I was still standing in front of her, trying to choose which of the chairs to sit in. She smiled at me and I felt a sudden dizzying rush, like maybe this was it, this was my life actually changing, probably forever.

"Thanks," I said. "Nice to meet you."

"Mm-hmm," she replied. She looked like she might laugh or say something else, but then she picked up her pen and went back to her drawing.

I sat at a marble-topped table in the corner. The red leather of the booth was worn, which made me feel a little better about the glamour of the whole thing. I tried not to stare at the girl still sketching at the marble host stand. Her dark hair was gathered into a ponytail that hung down her back. I wanted to tug on the end of it with my fingers, but my fingers didn't sparkle like freezer-burned Popsicles and I was not beautiful. I had freckles in the summer and a slightly upturned nose and my hair always looked like it had been slept on no matter what I did to it. I was, unfortunately, adorable.

"Alison," a tall man with a shiny bald head said as he walked toward me, interrupting my reverie. This was Brandon, I assumed. His forearms were covered in black ink. He was dressed in kitchen whites, although he was the general manager and not a chef.

"Nice to meet you," I said. "Thank you so much for meeting with me." I was already repeating myself. The immaculate but empty restaurant was warm. I felt like the air was on the verge of suffocating me.

"Mmm. Decent résumé," he said, looking at the paper I'd placed on the table. "And Steve said you were a hard worker. Not that a bookstore is anything like this," he said, using his chin to draw a half circle in the air.

I nodded.

"We're in a hotel, so we get lots of people from all over the place—Europeans, the occasional celebrity, though not as much lately—and we're near the park, so we also get oddballs wandering in to ask for money from guests or whatever. So we need someone who's comfortable in those situations. Kitchen usually closes at eleven. Host stays until midnight. Okay?"

"Okay," I repeated. Was he giving me the job?

"We usually don't hire people who haven't worked in the industry in the city before." He paused and looked at me straight on for the first time, like he was trying to read something in the top layer of my skin.

"I can only offer you the host job. No tips," he said. My stomach leaped.

"That's fine. I like front of house and I'm…" I stopped. "That's fine. I would love to work here."

"Okay. Good. We need a host who will actually stay a host and not leave in three weeks because the money is better as a server. It's twenty-five an hour, but, like I said, no tips."

I could feel my ears go hot. Twenty-five dollars an hour. That was almost twice as much as I'd made back home.

"I can give you four shifts a week right now, but the specific days will vary based on the week," he said.

"Thank you so much," I said.

"Can you start this Sunday? Mai will be here and she can train you. You probably saw her outside. Red hair."

"Sure." I bit the insides of my cheeks to prevent my mouth from widening into a grin.

"All right. We'll see you on Sunday, eight a.m. Dress code for hosts is black. No sneakers. Heels if you have them."

"Thank you so much," I said again, then stood up and shook his hand and walked as fast as I could back through the restaurant, the bar, the lobby, the front door, before he could change his mind. I walked so fast that the girl with the glittering fingers blurred by me. I didn't slow down enough to know whether she lifted her chin in farewell as I walked past her. The same patrons were still seated at the same tables, the server balancing coffee and tea on delicate white saucers like a scene from a French film I hadn't watched yet. I smiled wildly at the woman standing at the host stand outside, then pointed myself toward home. It had taken all of fifteen minutes and I was employed.

On my phone was a reply from Jen: *HI guess what Noah keeps asking about you! I just gave him your number. Want to come to a house party with us this Fri in Bushwick?*

My stomach did a little dip in a way that felt like *Oh my god.* Noah sounded like the name of a boat or a character in a movie or a boy from a small, liberal city who studied political science at a good college. My head still ached and sweat collected on the backs of my legs as I stood at the corner, waiting for the light to change, typing: *sounds good i'll be there.*

I walked up the apartment building's steep stairs, my phone like a good-luck charm in my sister's bright blue bag. I unlocked the door, and inside, it was empty. The balloon of excitement, high and tight in my chest, deflated. The apartment felt small and humid and I was frustrated; here I was, trying on a new life, and still, emptiness.

Emptiness was a disease in my family. My dad ran from it before my sister was born. He went to Nashville, my grandmother told us when we were girls, because...She'd never once finished that sentence. I always wondered how it might end. My mother tried to fill it up with smoke and sharp liquor until her body was too sick to fight it anymore. And my sister—she walked into the ocean and never came out.

I was seventeen and she was sixteen. I was working at the sports bar, partly so I could help our grandmother out with the bills, partly so I had somewhere to be besides our dark, quiet house. It was summer, our favorite time of the year, and instead of spending it with my sister, I was working, at the cove with friends, or asleep. I didn't notice that my sister was spending so much time at home, alone and quiet, until our grandmother asked if I would take her with me to do something fun.

"She's barely left her room since school let out," our grandmother whispered to me in the kitchen. "All she does is go to work, come home."

I assumed she was just tired. She had a job babysitting two boys, which sounded exhausting. That was the lie I told myself so I didn't have to ask her if everything was okay, admit that I was tired of missing out on the things all the other girls did, the girls who didn't have to spend so much of their time taking care of their younger sisters and grandmothers. My sister and I were so close in age, I was just barely the oldest, but I knew when the property taxes on my grandmother's house were due and I'd learned how to cook when her arthritis got bad. I paid the utility bill. I helped with my sister's homework, made sure she signed up for soccer in the spring. But now it was summer, and I wanted to drink beer on Jen's dad's boat and not care so much.

One night in July, I got back late from work and my sister wasn't in her twin bed in the room we shared. The bed was made up neatly, which was strange, but I was so tired that I could feel it in my eyelids. There was a big party on the beach that night, one I was annoyed I'd missed because the girl who was supposed to work the late shift had never shown up. I'd assumed my sister was there, by the ocean. I was right.

Nobody could say for sure what happened, if she went swimming on a dare or was drunk and stumbled into the water by mistake. My grandmother insisted it was a horrible accident. Nobody said what I knew, which was that she was so lonely that her fingertips felt numb. That I hadn't protected my sister from the current of emptiness, and its dark tendrils had wrapped around her ankles and pulled her away from me.

Since then, the long, hot days of summer had felt oppressive. The endless hours of daylight felt like a sick joke each year, but then again, she always felt closest in the summer. I stared at my ceiling and tried to will her back. It was a game I'd started playing years ago: If I closed my eyes and heard a bird chirp three times, my mom would come back. If I pinched the skin behind my knee as hard as I could for eighteen seconds, my sister would never have walked into the sea.

It had been a big deal when our mother died. We were moved to a new house to live with our grandmother, ushered hurriedly into our new life after our mom's death. She was so beautiful, so young, everyone said at her funeral. She was amazing at math and she drank so much. Jen's dad was the manager of the bank where she'd worked; they'd found bottles in drawers and toilet tanks after, bottles that had belonged to her, Jen whispered to me one night in high school when I slept over at her house.

When she died, people rushed in to fill the void. Our teachers were gentle with us; our friends' parents made sure we were invited to spend the night. But when my sister died, it was a loss that was all my own, and I was stunned by the unrelenting sting of it. Days went by, weeks, months, and years, and still, her absence was a sharp grain of grief that wouldn't dissolve. And I missed her just as badly in New York as I had in Awnor.

The next morning, I woke up with the hot sun and nothing to do. I didn't have my first shift at the restaurant until Sunday, didn't have the party in Bushwick until Friday, and already, I felt the ragged threads of me unraveling. I was a kid on summer break, friendless. I wanted to hold my breath underwater in a warm blue pool. I wanted to hide and wait for someone to find me. I wanted to watch lightning splinter the sky. I'd told myself before I left Awnor that I would become someone different, I would write and read and meet new people and look at art and do whatever it is people did when they had dreams and friends and apartments in big cities. But without anything to reel my time around, I felt adrift.

I got up and put on running clothes—black track shorts and a white T-shirt with yellowed pits—but when I reached the sidewalk, I felt too self-conscious to jog around all of the bright busy people walking to their jobs, so I bought coffee at a bodega and returned to sit on my fire escape with my book. When I heard something scrabbling and looked up to see a rat running up the metal laddered stairs, I went back inside and sat on my bed. I wondered if I hated New York. I listened hard for signs of life from my roommates but heard nothing. The sun didn't set until almost nine, and as the sky turned purple, I realized I hadn't spoken since ordering my coffee at the bodega the entire day. Not even a single *I'm fine, and you?*

"Hi," I said to my empty room. My voice sounded dry, and my stomach gurgled. I hadn't brushed my teeth or eaten. A coil of self-loathing moved like a wave inside me.

Once the sky got completely dark, I slid on my rubber flip-flops, brushed my teeth, and walked to the nearest grocery store. It felt good to leave the apartment. Good but not great. There were too many beautiful people on the sidewalk. It was almost a relief to walk into the fluorescent glare of the supermarket.

In the very front, there was a heated metal rack with plastic bags of rotisserie chickens sitting in their juices, orange stickers reading $4.99. I picked one up, paid, and walked home, where I sat on my floor and tore at the meat with my fingers. I ate one of the drumsticks. I ate the tiny wings. I ate until I found the wishbone. I had nobody to snap it in half with, so I made a wish with my left hand and a wish with my right hand and pulled the bone apart. It made a wet snap. My wishes weren't identical but they had the same gist. *Please, please, please let this not have been a huge mistake.*

I was nervous about having three roommates in a tiny apartment after living by myself for so long, but I still hadn't met any of them besides Marcus, who'd unlocked the door for me on the first day. He had a tiny black cherry tattooed on his cheekbone and didn't specify which of the three keys he handed me unlocked which of the three dead bolts on the front door, our front door. It was so strange that we shared a door and I didn't know his last name.

I'd thought I'd known loneliness living by myself in my dead grandmother's house, but this was almost worse, knowing there were three other beating hearts smiling and brushing their teeth and falling asleep under the same roof as me. It was eerie to see the coffee maker turned on or a wet towel hanging in the bathroom, a ghostly kind of intimacy.

The night of the party, I willed myself into a less horrible mood. I unpacked my clothes from the trash bags, hung them on a metal wardrobe rack I'd rescued from outside someone's stoop. I'd moved to the city to be something other than alone, and now I was going to a party. It was a Friday and I had a bedroom of my own and a job at a restaurant where celebrities sometimes maybe ate and I was fine. I would be fine.

I got to the address Jen had texted, a nondescript concrete block on Bushwick Avenue. The front door was propped open, and a piece of notebook paper was taped to it with *Hey, neighbors, party in 301! Stop by!* scribbled on it in blue pen, a smiley face drawn beneath. I walked up the stairs and heard house music spilling from an open door. There were red string lights flashing from the ceiling and bodies everywhere moving up and down in waves, undulating to the music. I walked in, did a lap around the room, and got squished between the fridge in the kitchen and a very tall guy with a silver cross dangling from his left ear.

"Excuse me!" I yelled, but he didn't hear me. I pulled out my phone to see if Jen had texted again with any details about where exactly they were. She had not. I hoped they hadn't left already. I opened my Notes app and pretended to type something important. Just then, a hand wrapped around my wrist and pulled me away from the fridge. I looked up and it was him, Noah, with eyelashes that were so dark and long they looked fake.

"Thank god!" I yelled over the music. "I thought maybe I was at the wrong party."

"Unfortunately not!" Noah yelled back, pulling me onto the dance floor. Jen squealed when she saw me and handed me her drink.

"I thought you weren't coming!" she said. "Have mine! I need to pee!"

I took a sip. It was tequila and Sprite, a not-bad combination. Noah grabbed my hand and twirled me around, a dance maneuver that did not match the staticky, electronic music but made my cheeks get hot in a way that felt good. I knew almost exactly nothing about this person except that he was beautiful, tall, and slender like a ballerina, with arms that felt strong around mine as we danced. His dark hair looked purposely shaggy and the hoop through his nose seemed to point directly toward his full lips, red like they'd just been bitten.

His hand was on my waist and he bent toward me. He said something I couldn't hear but I smiled and did a little fake laugh as if I could, and then he put his thumb on my bottom lip and slid it slowly between my teeth. Every cell in my body felt like it had turned into a dolphin, a diamond, a dark and endless sky. Then he said, as if it were the most certain thing in the world, "Let's go."

"Wait," I said as he led me toward the exit, our sweaty

fingers interlaced. "I should tell Jen bye." It felt like everything was happening slow and fast at the same time. Hadn't I just crossed the Williamsburg Bridge, dragged trash bags full of clothes up my dirty apartment stairs? Hadn't I just donated the detritus of my grandmother's house to Goodwill? I was just waking up from a long nap. I was still getting my bearings, walking off my sea legs.

"Jen left, like, five minutes after you got here," he replied as he pushed through the door. Then we were on the sidewalk, the night air cool on my bare legs. I checked my phone, pretended like I had something to do. I felt very alone all of a sudden, knowing Jen had left already. I wasn't sure how to proceed. Noah had walked out of the party with conviction but now we were just standing in the middle of a busy sidewalk in Brooklyn.

"I've actually got to get going. I have to work tomorrow," I said, a lie.

"Okay," Noah said. He didn't seem disappointed or surprised. I felt annoyed. I wanted to feel him wanting me. I wanted him to bat me between his paws.

"Did you call an Uber?" he asked.

I pretended to check my phone again. "Yeah," I said. I didn't know why I felt the need to lie. I couldn't afford an Uber. I could barely afford the subway. "But it's still, like, ten minutes away. You don't have to wait."

"I'll wait."

We leaned against the building, shoulders not touching. The empty space between our arms felt like a minus sign, and my stomach turned. I wondered how long he would stay before he realized my ride wasn't coming. I pretended to check my phone again.

Noah turned his head toward me and I looked up at him. He had full lips and his eyes were so dark, they looked like ink or coffee with nothing in it. His stubble was a light shadow across his face, and I knew without touching it that it would feel abrasive, like dry sand. I was thinking the word *abrasive* when he bent down and kissed me. It wasn't a nice kiss. It was hard, and I'd been right about the stubble. He bit the bottom of my lip, grabbed the back of my neck.

"Come home with me." His eyes were an impossible shade darker.

"I have work," I lied again, but I wanted to know what his lips would feel like everywhere else. I looked down and was surprised to find he was wearing loafers with his beat-up, perfect blue jeans. I could almost see my reflection in his shiny shoes.

"Come home with me," he said again. I wondered if I could will myself into love, or something adjacent, with Noah, fall in with Jen's rich and beautiful friends, attach myself to them, the easy way they seemed to glide through life, guided by a mechanism I didn't understand but that could make my life easier, peopled: group texts, brunch plans, maybe even a job in an office. A life with less friction.

"Okay," I said.

A car pulled up just then, the Uber he had ordered for himself. It was a black SUV. I realized then that he'd known the whole time that I hadn't called a car, that I would kiss him back, that I would say okay. I resented that he was right but crawled into the car behind him, buckled my seat belt, rested my palm on the top of his thigh. My fingertips slid closer to his lap each time the car came to a bumpy halt or swerved around a biker. I could feel him tense and stiffen. I liked that I could do that, alter the shape of him.

It was such a long drive to Midtown, which was all sky-scrapers and Starbucks. I was drunk, and we were still in the car, and I said, "You look like a bartender," and he laughed. I said, "I miss my sister," and he laughed at that too.

"Everyone misses someone," he replied, and I didn't correct him, didn't say that my sister was no longer a someone but a gray headstone adorned with wilting grocery-store flowers, or maybe a fleck of sea glass on a long sandy beach.

Noah's apartment was clean and spare. There was a painting on the wall that looked like horses running away from something, but I couldn't tell for sure. It was all in red.

"Drink?" he asked.

I nodded. The last time I'd slept with someone was the summer before, almost a year ago. I tried to remember his name. He was visiting Awnor from somewhere out west, kept saying how he loved how slowly people talked, how he loved the warm ocean, didn't even care that it was gray. Our town's existence balanced on the wobbly axis of seasonal tourism, the benevolence of strangers. Almost every word he said made me hate him. He did not make me come and when I realized after

I got home the next morning that I'd left an earring in his hotel room, I'd thrown its lonely remainder away. It was cheap anyway, a flimsy thing from a superstore.

Noah handed me something dark in a heavy glass. I started to say that I didn't drink whiskey and then stopped. Instead I poured the whole thing down my throat in one awful gulp and grimaced.

"Easy," he said, laughing.

"I hate whiskey," I said. I was sitting on his kitchen counter. He kissed me, used his knee to part my legs, hungry. I was too. I took my shirt off and he did the same. I liked watching him follow me. I felt hot and liquid, although he had barely touched me anywhere but my lips.

He unbuckled his expensive-looking belt, unzipped his jeans, and rocked into me, then carried me to the long leather couch that sat in front of an enormous television. It was cool on my bare back. He wrapped a hand around my throat, loosely, and I said, "Tighter," and he gasped, said, *"Fuck,"* and then it was that unfurling, sparks dripping from my toes, my body expanding everywhere and back into myself, and I heard my breath, and I bit his ear.

Afterward, I put my shorts and my T-shirt back on. I hadn't taken my boots off.

"Sorry I put my shoes on your couch. And I actually do have to work tomorrow."

I was surprised by how very suddenly I wanted to be in my own apartment, showered and alone. I did not want to sleep in his sheets or spend even one minute wondering when they'd last been washed, and the red painting of the maybe-horses fleeing was giving me a bad feeling.

"Whatever you say." He shrugged. "Let's do this again soon. I like you. You're different," he said, and I tried to smile, tried to ignore the feeling of wanting to roll my eyes. *Different.* What a meaningless thing to say.

"Sure, maybe. My Uber is here."

"Right," Noah said.

I checked my phone as I walked out into the cool night air. It was four in the morning. I felt a bit of wonder at being out so late in a big city, and then I felt stupid for feeling special. It would take an hour to walk home.

I got a slice of pepperoni at a place called, satisfyingly, Hot Pizza. I ate it while I walked. I'd wanted him, Noah. I'd wanted him; I'd gotten him. I was whatever I wanted to be now, every single thing. But had I wanted him or had I just wanted him to claw at me, scrape off the downy fuzz of my loneliness, remind me of my hot beating heart?

I texted Jen: *what do you think about Noah?*

She didn't respond and a few blocks later, I typed *I'm not sure about him,* as if I hadn't needed her to answer the question at all. I backspaced the letters without sending the message and took a deep breath in. Noah had a whole apartment to himself, something that seemed almost unfathomable to me. I tried to imagine myself in it. I didn't like his whiskey or his cold leather couch. He had laughed at every joke I'd attempted, but hadn't his laughter sounded kind of hollow? My head was thick with whiskey and sex and an unfamiliar place.

❧

I was sweat-sticky and annoyed when I finally turned down the block toward my apartment. As I rummaged through my bag for the clunky gold key to the front door that always seemed to get lost in my tangle of wallet, phone, keys, I saw something flash in the air. It was like a scrap of fog or a shadow, silver and hazy and floating near the door of my building, right above the buzzer. I got closer, my hand still in my bag, my legs moving like they belonged to a different body.

It looked like a ghost. A ghost in the shape of a fish.

I closed my eyes. It was late. I was kind of drunk still. But when I opened my eyes, the ghostly figure was still there, floating in the dark. I turned my head away, unlocked the front door. I was surprised to find that my fingers were trembling. A ribbon of adrenaline was unspooling in me. I could hear my blood roaring in my ears as I stopped in the doorway. I was afraid to turn back, to look again, to think about the impossibility of the thought that had just flashed through my head.

Why did the ghost fish floating in the air remind me so much of my sister?

It wasn't real. Of course it wasn't. My sister was dead, and fish didn't float silver in the dark night air. It was the whiskey or the fact that it was nearing dawn and I needed, desperately, to sleep. Or maybe loneliness wasn't growing on me but

winding its bruised arms around my brain. I walked up the
stairs and the boots I was wearing made my footsteps loud. It
sounded like there were two or three of me echoing through
the building.

᯽

The apartment was as eerily silent as always. I moved as if I
were in a library, showered without playing music from my
phone like I used to back home, making my footsteps as quiet
as I could. I lay on my bed, which I'd finally made up with
too-big sheets from my grandmother's house. The light was
dark and blue. I closed my eyes but my brain felt buzzy, too
full, confused, so I got up to get some water from the kitchen.
There were no glasses in the apartment, something that had
initially struck me as very artsy and was now just annoying, so
I pulled down an empty washed-out pickle jar from the cabinet
and filled it up from the tap. I took a sip and tried to will my
racing heart to calm down.

"There you are."

I dropped the pickle jar and it clattered into the metal basin
of the sink, miraculously remaining intact. I turned toward the
voice, a girl around my age with bleached-white hair that was
almost silver in the dim light.

"Sorry!" The girl laughed. I tried to laugh with her but
couldn't quite manage it. "I didn't mean to scare you," she said.
"I'm Greta."

Her skin was bright white too, almost translucent. The

door across the living room from mine was ajar and I could see the rosy glow of twinkle lights. I wondered if she was nocturnal. She looked a bit vampiric, in a pretty way.

I picked up the pickle jar from where I'd dropped it. My hands were still shaking. I turned back around to face her.

"Hi. I'm Alison."

"I'm sorry we haven't met yet," Greta said. "Do you hate us? I hope you don't hate us."

"What? No," I replied, feeling self-conscious.

"Good," she said. "Marcus said he met you when you moved in. And he can just be . . . very Marcus. But we love him. And we all work weird hours. I didn't want you to think we were avoiding you. We're nice."

"I didn't think that," I said. It had never occurred to me that they were purposely avoiding me. I almost wished that were the case, that I precipitated any kind of emotion or action in the people who lived under the same roof as me. Being something, causing something, even if it was bad, felt better than being totally forgotten. But I'd probably never be part of Greta's *we*. When Greta said, *We're nice,* she would never mean me. She would never say to someone, *Alison can just be . . . very Alison. But we love her.*

"Good. I'm sure we'll all hang out sometime." She smiled. "It really is nice to meet you."

I stretched a smile across my face and refilled the jar with water. It was silent save for the sound of water from the tap drumming against the metal basin of the kitchen sink.

"Are you okay?" Greta asked.

I didn't know how to tell her, this stranger I lived with, that I had just seen a ghost that was a fish that also bore an inexplicable but visceral resemblance to my dead sister. I didn't know how to tell her that my sister was dead, as was my grandmother, as was my mother, that I was our family's only remnant and it really sucked sometimes to be so alone. Also, did she happen to know someone named Noah, and was it a terrible idea for me to keep sleeping with him?

"Fine. Just tired."

"Okay," she said, making the word a whole sentence, as if she were on the verge of saying something else. I turned around.

"It's nice to meet you. Good night," I said. I walked into my bedroom and closed the door. I could already feel my eyes getting hot. Why had I done that? Why hadn't I let Greta say whatever she'd been about to say, let it melt into a late-night chat? I could have told her everything and she could've told me I was in the right place, that I was home, wasn't I.

When my sister died, the police came in the buttery light of the morning. They came with sirens off and lights on, the red and blue of their patrol cars bleeding weakly into the morning air. I was seventeen, I didn't know anything, but I knew my sister was not in her bed and that when the police come with sirens off and lights on, something irreparable has happened. The yellow light and the blue light and the red light spilled through the curtainless windows over my sister's empty bed and I imagined walking down our long dirt driveway to the highway and lying down on the uneven asphalt, waiting for a truck with eighteen wheels to flatten me into the ground. I knew that would hurt less than sirens off, lights on, men with guns at their hips and mouths puckered with pretend sympathy.

The knock at the door, the sound of dread. The slow shuffle of my grandmother's bare feet. I squeezed my eyes shut so hard, a tear spilled out of my right eye, the eye closer to my sister's bed. I got up, my body heavy and unreal, and turned down the hall. My grandmother was opening the screen door. Two men were speaking, words drifting toward me: *Late last night, party, ocean, nobody knows, found her. Floating.* The word *floating* felt like it had been flung across the room and down my throat, making me gag. I ran for the kitchen and threw up in the sink. I heard my grandmother say, "Thank you, Officers," and I hated her for that. I turned on the tap in the sink, watched my bile spiral down the drain. Although our mother had died when we were young, I hadn't spent much time considering the actual physical reality of death until that very moment. My hand did not look real. My sister would never use this sink again, never turn the tap on to fill up a glass of water. My sister no longer needed a glass of water. My sister no longer needed to borrow my favorite jeans. My sister. I threw up again. The tap was still running.

Once, my mother had taken my sister and me for an early-morning walk on the beach. As we crested the dunes, the sand orangey in the sunrise glow, we smelled something tangy and overripe. I felt the inside of my nose twitch. Hundreds of horseshoe crabs dotted the shore. They were eerily still, their spiny tails askew.

"Oh, how sad," our mother said. "They're dead."

"What's dead?" my sister asked.

"It means they're gone," my mom had said. Our shoes were in our hands and she drew a line in the cold wet sand with her toe. "Their bodies are here, but they're nothing now."

I turned the kitchen tap off. I listened to my grandmother cry in the next room. I would not be angry with her for saying thank you to the policemen who came to tell us the best person I knew was dead. I would go to my grandmother, put a warm hand on her thin back. I would read a poem at my sister's funeral and graduate from high school. I would clock in to my shifts at work and do the grocery shopping. But I decided to be nothing. My body was here, like the horseshoe crabs on the beach, but if she couldn't be anything, I would be nothing too.

Except now, I wasn't nothing. I was in an apartment in a city. I was trying something new.

My room was usually dark as ink at night, but out of the corner of my eye, I saw something was different. A weak silvery glow leaked in through the window. I didn't so much walk toward it as let myself be dragged by some weird emotion I couldn't parse. Dread and hope. Fear and love.

Outside, above the fire escape, the ghost fish floated in the air. I opened the window for her to come in. She smelled like my sister, the subtle sweetness of cheap powdery deodorant and the dryer sheets our grandmother used. Her fins and tail floated behind her as if she were swimming through water, not the warm, still air of my bedroom. I shivered as she inspected my stack of books, then drifted toward my rack of clothes. The air in my room felt cool now, a chill from the night, the open window. I didn't close it, I didn't want to trap her, except of course I did. She stopped in front of the blue-sequined Coach bag hanging on the end of my silver clothing rack and turned toward me. I was not breathing. I was standing by the window, the pickle jar full of water in my hands. That jar, that water, my standing in the kitchen just a minute before, had happened in a different world.

She came close to me and I could feel one of her fins brush against my cheek. As she moved, her light became weaker. She floated in front of my face and stilled herself. We stared at each other, my sister-ghost-fish and I. She dimmed again in the black air, her light leaking away like death. A strangled sob moved through the room, disturbing the silence like a rock to a wave. It came from me. I felt my chest contract, preparing to crack as her light got dimmer. Her silver was now gray. Would I lose her again? I could feel grief in my ribs, in my lungs, all that nothing gasping inside me.

"Don't go," I said. I could feel my face getting wet and hot. I didn't want to scare her, but a sharp want lunged through me. I needed her to stay.

Her fish eyes darted around the room. They landed on the

jar in my hands, still full of cool water from the sink. She dived through the air toward it. When her ghostly form touched the water, her scales exploded into color: orange, like the sky furiously coming to life in the morning.

All at once, I was very aware that the ghost of my dead sister now existed in an apartment full of strangers. It seemed absolutely critical that nobody saw her, nobody laid eyes on her except me. I understood, the way one understands that the sun is yellow, that her existence now hinged on my ability to keep her safe from the world. She waved a fin in the air as her fish eyes blinked closed. I placed the jar carefully on the windowsill by my bed and sat next to her. I would not take my eyes away from her. She swam to the bottom of the jar and lay there. I knew she was sleeping. I could feel a stillness inside of me, the kind I hadn't felt since before she'd drowned.

I studied each of her scales, slotted together like puzzle pieces. She was so bright. I could see her tiny fish body breathing in and out. Couldn't I? My nose almost touched the glass of the jar and I tried to keep as still and quiet as I could. Once upon a time, my sister had hair so light it was almost the color of a blank piece of paper. Her skin flushed pink the moment the sun touched it. Now she was a fish asleep in a jar on a windowsill in a city her human body had never gotten to visit. I felt guilt like vomit in the back of my throat. I mouthed the words *I'm sorry.* I would wait until she woke up and I would never stop saying *I'm sorry. I love you.*

I woke up gasping like I'd swum underwater and stayed too long. I was still sitting upright, slumped against the wall, facing my sister. She was just as bright orange as the night before, and awake now, floating in the jar, her long, delicate fins waving back and forth.

"Can you hear me?" I asked. She bobbed up and down as if she were nodding yes. I was desperate to hear her voice. My hands clutched the windowsill, my skin was oily and unwashed, and up and down she bobbed, my sister-ghost-fish, my impossible wish. She opened her fish mouth and a bubble floated to the top of the pickle jar.

"It's okay," I replied. I didn't know what else to say.

I had always believed in ghosts. I believed in ghosts, and in something after, and in not knowing. The day of sirens off, lights on, I'd believed in praying to god that my worst nightmare had not come true, and then I'd believed in wishing on every star that I'd *survive* my nightmare coming true. I believed in everything: in hoping and wishing and pleading. How could I not? And there was something real but also magic, or magic but also real, in my tiny room that still smelled of chicken and stale sweat. My eyes burned like I'd opened them in the brine of the ocean, but I hadn't been swimming since before my sister had gone. And now she was here, I could see her sister-ghost-fish body through my salt-burned eyes. She was floating in the jar right in front of me, the color of a clementine. She was waving *Hello, I'm back.*

One of the therapists I'd seen after my sister died but before my grandmother did had told me to have difficult conversations while doing an activity of some kind, like walking. Something about eye contact and anxiety. So I asked my sister if she wanted to go for a walk. She bobbed up and down, something that I knew in my resurrected-sister brain meant yes.

The streets were quieter than usual and the morning light made the city seem softer. I realized it was Saturday. I'd found the lid of the pickle jar, sticky, in a kitchen drawer. I scrubbed it clean, and in my room, I'd screwed the top on, wrapped a sweater around my sister in her jar, and placed her in a canvas tote bag from a grocery store that said *thank you* in three different fonts. I hung the bag from my shoulder. My hand rested gently on her jar through the fabric. I could feel its round glass shape through the sweater and I held her as still as I could.

"Where should we go?" I whispered, trying not to move my lips. I didn't want passersby to think I was talking to myself. She didn't answer. I walked toward the subway station on Essex. There was almost nobody on the sidewalk and the absence felt conspicuous. In front of a dark, mirrored storefront, I gently unwound the sweater from around my sister's jar, lifted her from the tote bag, and held her up. I could see my reflection in the window, a normal-looking girl holding up a pickle jar, empty but for the water from the kitchen sink. I looked down at the jar in my hands, my sister swimming a graceful loop, then back up at the reflection: just me and the jar. I put her back in my bag, dug my fingernails into my palm until I felt a sting.

"What's happening?" I whispered to my sister.

She did not whisper back.

At the subway station, I swiped us through the turnstile. The first train that arrived was Brooklyn-bound. I sat on an orange bench and put the bag holding my sister-ghost-fish on my lap. Each time I looked in the bag to make sure she was still there, floating, my stomach flipped. I was so afraid she might disappear. The subway rumbled across the Williamsburg Bridge, over the East River, which looked blue and gentle from this far away. The car was miraculously empty, so I took the jar out of my bag and held it up to the window so she could see the water. I didn't like looking at the ocean, being anywhere near any kind of water. It wasn't that I was afraid of it but that I knew the truth of it, how easily it could take. But now my sister was back and it was like we were caught in a tide carrying us to the sea.

The conductor said, "Myrtle Avenue," then "Broadway Junction," and we stood up, walked off the train, my hand at her side, standing on the smoky platform. Another train and then we were coasting again above water, ocean that was endless and murky.

Outside, it was warm, almost muggy. We walked across a busy street, past a parking lot with cracked pavement. A rat rustled through trash cans that had tipped over in the middle of the sidewalk, but I could smell the ocean and it smelled like home.

I could feel my sister swimming in circles in her pickle jar, the water sloshing back and forth as we drew closer. And then I saw it, the enormous gray-blue sea. I kicked my sneakers off as we stepped onto the sand, a habit from back home, even though it was cold under my feet in the morning light. I sat down close to the ocean. Its waves sounded louder than the ones back home somehow, like thunder. A city sea.

I took my sister out of the tote bag and made sure the top was still on tight. It worried me what might happen if I fell and the glass shattered or if the top came undone and even a drop of water leaked out. I wished she could speak to me. I was desperate to know what she needed, what the rules of her new existence were. I dug a shallow hole and put her jar in it so it could stand up straight. She bobbed up and down in the pickle jar, nodding yes and yes and yes toward the ocean.

"The waves are bigger than I thought they would be," I said.

The last time my sister went to the beach, she didn't come back. It both surprised me and didn't that she seemed happy here.

"Does it scare you?" I asked.

Her scales looked even brighter than they had in my room. The sun made her glow. Her reflection hadn't shown up in the dark glass of the storefront. But her eyes, her fins, her bright orange scales—she so decisively *was*. Wasn't she?

"It scares me. It makes me feel lonely," I said.

She stilled her fish body, looked at me with her fish eyes.

The only other person on the beach was a man with a gray beard walking his dog. I wondered if he believed in ghosts. The hot sun glinted off the water and was already turning the tops of my arms pink. The sand was warmer now, soft beneath my feet. I was so happy I thought I might dissolve into a million pieces, an ocean of, oh my god, my sister.

The next day was my first day of work. The inside of my stomach rippled with dread. I didn't want to leave my sister, but I couldn't bring her with me. I thought for a moment about not showing up, finding another job in a couple of weeks; it was a big city, I could manage. But I would have to pay rent soon, buy toothpaste. So I dressed, to code, in dark black jeans and my nicest flats. It was early and the light was soft and diffuse through the window. I put a little extra water in my sister's jar and left her on the sill.

"Please don't go," I said. "I promise I'll be back."

I felt newly alone on the sidewalk, my bag light without the jar inside it. I chewed a stick of gum, picked at a loose piece of skin on the cuticle of my right thumb, and listened to music loud in my headphones as I walked the twenty minutes to work. It was already hot, and I had forgotten to put on deodorant when I was getting dressed. I wanted to stop to buy a stick, but I didn't have much money left, and Brandon hadn't said when or how much I'd be paid for training shifts. I changed my mind every block—*I will stop; I won't stop*—but the next time I passed a CVS, I ran in. I could already feel half-moons of sweat through my cardigan.

It was always terrible, being the newest person in a restaurant. I hated beginnings—pilot episodes of television shows, first pages of books—almost as much as I hated endings. All I wanted was to sit in my room and watch my sister bob up and down in her jar. I wanted nearness, not excruciating distance. I wondered if the other people at the restaurant would be nice, if they would like me. I wondered if I would see the girl from last time, the girl with the rings that glittered in the light and the dark ponytail.

I could see the twinkly lights of the restaurant strung above the sidewalk from a block away. The wooden podium outside looked like something a teacher in a small blue schoolhouse might have used long ago, and as I drew closer, I saw a piece of paper with handwritten reservations lying atop. I wondered if everything about this place was like that, practiced whimsy and mechanical quirk. I missed my sister already.

A woman with hair dyed cherry red sat behind the podium. She wore a black dress, clogs, and the most perfect shade of plum lipstick. I wanted to ask her if she knew the poem, the one about the plums and the icebox.

"Are you Mai?" I asked instead.

She looked at me like I was trying to lick her.

"Sorry, I'm the new host," I said quickly.

"I didn't know we had a new host," she replied, arching an eyebrow. "But yeah, I'm Mai."

"Oh, um, sorry about that," I said. I wondered how many times I would say *sorry* in the next eight hours. "Brandon said he would tell you. Is there somewhere I can put my bag?"

"Brandon is an idiot about the schedule," she said, rolling her eyes. "Sure. Follow me."

I walked behind Mai up the marble stairs and into the dark lobby. There was a small opening beside the bar with a heavy wooden door.

"This is the hutch," she said, holding the door open. Inside, it was empty and even darker than the lobby, a large closet lined on the left with walnut-brown shelves that held folded napkins, trays of silverware, salt and pepper shakers, silver bowls with packets of sugar. A bulky computer with a receipt printer attached by a tangle of wires was wedged precariously onto one of the shelves. On the right side, Mai explained, was the pass, a small opening between the hutch and the bar where the bartender put drinks for servers to distribute to guests. I wondered if the hutch might be the secret annex, the servers' clubhouse, the place where drinks were drunk at the end of the shift, where vapes were vaped, after-work plans made.

"You can put your bag on the hook there," Mai finished.

She turned and went out the swinging door. I hung my bag up quickly and pushed through the door, scanned the lobby and restaurant, but there was no one at the marble host stand inside, no servers with long ponytails and rings on their fingers.

Mai was at the bar talking to a man holding a silver cocktail shaker.

I'd worked in enough restaurants to know that, from the most suspicious C-rated sports bar to the fanciest steak house, the bartender was the locus of every establishment. Bartenders had a frisson of heat, energy, something to do with how they spoke, moved their hands, existed. They always seemed to get away with flirting with guests, showing up a few minutes late, even asking one of the line chefs for a snack right in the middle of a shift. I couldn't help eyeing him with caution.

"Hey," I said, returning to Mai's side.

"Alison, Mike. Mike, Alison," Mai said. She was not a person of many words, I was learning. Mike nodded his chin at me by way of greeting, so neither was he, apparently. His forearm flexed as he did some kind of acrobatic thing with the silver cocktail shaker.

"Watch out for this one," he said to me, tilting his head toward Mai. Men always said that about women when they had no idea what they were talking about. Mai rolled her eyes.

"Let's go back outside," she said.

We walked through the lobby, half full of people glued to their phones and laptops. I had never worked in a restaurant attached to a hotel before. It was a strange, quiet atmosphere. I was happy that the host stand was outside in the bright morning sun, but training was always excruciating. I hated having to follow someone around hoping that they would explain what I needed to do instead of chatting about inane restaurant politics or giving me the new-girl silent treatment.

I'd predicted Mai would go the silent route, so I was pleasantly surprised when she thoroughly explained how we took reservations: old-school, penciling names and times into a leather-bound book.

"We don't do online reservations. People have to call and speak to a real person. Or they can just walk in." She paused. "Most people just walk in. We aren't very busy these days."

We stood shoulder to shoulder in the morning sun, saying *Hi, Hello, How many?* The tables outside filled up, guests drawn to the seats outdoors in the sunlight, and the time passed quickly, to my surprise. Eventually Mai said, "What do you want for your training meal?"

"Can I order from the menu?" I asked.

"Yes. It's your training meal," she repeated slowly.

"Um, I'll have the cheeseburger," I said.

"Okay." She walked up the stairs and into the restaurant and I was on my own. I sat a family of four who looked sweaty and exhausted from a day wandering around Manhattan and then a couple who said they lived across the street. Mai returned with a brown cardboard takeout container.

"Here's your food. You can go."

"Are you sure?" I hadn't been there for a full shift yet, and I wanted all the hours I could get, but I also wanted home, sister, windowsill.

"Yeah."

"Do you know how many training shifts I'll have?"

She shrugged. "No idea. I'm a host just like you, babe."

I walked straight back to my apartment, my heart crashing in my chest, my mouth dry. The entire day had felt weird, surreal. It wasn't a hard job and it paid more than I'd expected, but something about the unfamiliarity of it, the inscrutable rules of a new workplace, made me feel like the borders of my existence were wavering—like if I never returned, nobody would notice. And the restaurant itself wasn't quite what I'd thought it would be. The furniture was expensive and the linen was too, and they used fancy, boutique brands of coffee and juice, but it was golden only at the edges. Up close, everything had a sheen of wear; the cracks in the red vinyl booths were held together with duct tape, the linen napkins held old stains. It had the air of a place that had seen its golden age and was quietly decaying, waiting for someone to put it out of its misery. I wondered if it would exist if it didn't have the hotel to lean on.

But mostly, I didn't care. I wanted to be home. I was terrified that I'd been gone too long, that when I returned the pickle jar on my windowsill would be empty. The walk was excruciating. When I got back to the apartment, Greta was making spaghetti on the stove and I flew by her with barely a nod of acknowledgment, too anxious to care that I was being rude. I watched my hand open my door slowly, like I was in a horror film, but my room was soft and bright in the afternoon sun and my sister was waiting for me, still orange, still the most ordinary-looking fish, and yet still unmistakably my sister. I sat down hard on my bed and realized I was exhausted.

"I'm so glad you're here," I said. She bobbed up and down in her pickle jar—yes, yes, she was glad too.

I kicked my shoes off and lay down on my bed, eggs Benedict–flecked outfit, sweaty cardigan, and all. I was in a hard, dreamless sleep before I realized I had even closed my eyes. When I woke up, the sun was going down, milky pink light was creeping into my room, and I'd barely said a word since I'd gotten home.

It was embarrassing, how much I dreaded running into my roommates. I seldom saw anything but a hint of them, and now it felt like I'd been there too long to really become friends with them or even properly introduce myself in a way that wasn't awkward. I'd thought maybe they didn't interact much either, but that couldn't be true because I could hear, at that very moment, laughter in the living space outside my bedroom door. I stood there, eavesdropping, trying to determine what my roommates might be like. I couldn't. I looked at my sister.

"Now would be a good time for some words of encouragement or something," I said. She waved a fin toward the door and I rolled my eyes. She'd always been less afraid of human beings. I was quiet and protective; she liked existing around the noise and light of others.

I turned the doorknob quietly. A trio of people were sitting in the living room, the furnishings of which consisted of a futon, a plastic Adirondack chair, and a three-legged yellow stool on top of which sat a bowl packed with weed.

The guy who unlocked the door for me the day I'd moved in, Marcus, sat on the red futon. I was pretty sure he worked nights, though I couldn't imagine what he did. Greta sat on the floor, her long silver hair almost grazing it, next to a boy covered in strawberry-colored freckles.

All three of their heads swiveled toward me, a family of foxes anticipating a predator.

"Oh, shit," Marcus said, "I keep forgetting Ty moved out."

I opened my mouth, then closed it again. I wasn't sure how to respond.

"I'm sorry that Marcus is a dick. We're really high," said Greta. Her hair looked like it should have stars woven through it. "Also, I'm Greta. In case you forgot."

The boy smattered with freckles looked at me without saying anything, his thin lips in a line exactly between a smile and a frown.

"That's Leo," Greta said, gesturing toward him. "He's shy."

Leo nodded.

"Nice to meet y'all. You all." I swallowed. "I was just going to take a shower." I slowly started moving around the group, toward the bathroom. I felt, stupidly, like I was circling them.

"Nice to see you again," Greta said.

"Word," said Marcus.

"I like your toenail polish," Leo whispered as I walked

away. They were painted pale pink, my toes, like the inside of a seashell. I smiled.

When I got out of the shower, wrapped in a giant blue-and-white beach towel, the cheapest option at the Duane Reade around the block, I heard them laughing again. The bathroom was rainforest-steamy. It didn't have a fan or a window and was always at least a little damp. I walked out of the bathroom and could feel my wet hair dripping down my back and onto the floor behind me, leaving a trail like the shine of a snail.

"Do you want to smoke?" asked Greta.

"Sure." I held my towel closed, sat down, and accepted the bowl from her outstretched hand. I wondered if my sister could hear us from her jar in the next room. I wasn't sure if she'd ever smoked weed. If she had, she hadn't told me.

"Wait, have you done this before?" Marcus asked. "Greta, show her how or she's going to waste it."

"I've smoked weed before," I said. I could feel my eyes narrow. Marcus was the kind of person who had probably transcended popular in high school, with his skateboard-battered Vans and heavy-lidded eyes. He was too effortless to care about popularity. I'd always wanted those guys to like me but never knew where to begin. Now I lived with one of them.

I inhaled deeply, wanting it to be obvious that I'd done this before—smoked—but not wanting to look like I was showing off. It occurred to me that I was half naked in my towel and my hair was still dripping water down my back and that I hadn't yet heard Leo speak above a whisper.

"Okay, okay," Marcus said, holding two hands up, palms facing me, like a crossing guard. "She's a cool girl."

I laughed. It felt good to laugh. It felt good to be in a towel, hair wet, sitting on the floor in my living room. I passed the bowl to Leo and he inhaled deeply, then exhaled the smoke in perfect Os, like a pool shark celebrating a victory.

"Whoa," I said.

Greta laughed. Leo smiled.

"Leo, stop showing off, man," Marcus said, but he was laughing too.

"Okay, we absolutely have to go or we're going to be beyond late," Greta said, and the threesome stood and collected their lighter and baggies. Marcus walked to the fridge and took out a case of PBR.

I stood up carefully, clutching my towel around me.

"Thanks," I said.

"So nice to see your face again!" Greta said, and she flung her arms around me, squeezed, then was across the room, taking a beer from Marcus's outstretched hand, opening the front door. I hadn't been touched since the party in Bushwick, the night after, and her arms felt like a benevolent planet, circling me.

"Nice to meet you," Leo said seriously and held out his open hand. I put mine in his, like he meant to bring me with him wherever he was going. I held on for a second too long before I realized he'd meant to shake.

"Oh!" I laughed again. I was glad I was already feeling high, floating above embarrassment. My body was warm. I squeezed his hand before letting go. He smiled a smile that matched the warmth inside me and I tried to find words to ask if we could, I don't know, be friends? Go for a long walk and hold hands?

"Have fun" was the only thing I managed to squeak out as Marcus and Leo and Greta waved goodbye, disappearing through the apartment's door.

My phone was on my bed, face up, where I'd left it. There was a text from an unknown caller lighting the screen and I knew who it was before I picked the phone up: *drinks?* he'd written. And a second text: *it's noah btw*. I found it annoying that he texted with uncapitalized letters, like a wannabe e. e. cummings. The warmth evaporated from my body.

I held my phone up to my sister's jar and made a face. I had, of course, told her everything already: the purple club, the make-out in Bushwick, the weird horse painting on his wall. Her fish face puckered and she bobbed left and right in her jar, a gesture I interpreted as *no. Sorry can't tonight,* I responded. *Have to work tomorrow*—which was not, in fact, a lie. He responded right away: *lol.*

"He's not a very serious person, is he?" I said to my sister. It was a rhetorical question in that she couldn't, or didn't, respond.

I put on a big T-shirt, climbed into bed, opened my laptop, and started another episode of *Golden Girls*. We were already on the second season. I didn't want to go out with Noah, but I had felt a twinge of something, watching Greta and Marcus and Leo leave for a night out. I glanced at my sister. *You are not alone,* her fins seemed to signal as she bobbed in her jar, eyes glued to my laptop.

✦

The next week: sister, sister, sister. We were rarely apart, and I could hardly breathe when I was away from her. I fidgeted behind the host stand at work, anxious to go home as soon as I arrived. The whole world looked raw, unreal. How were all these buildings still standing, why were all these people streaming in and out of them like ants, when my once-dead sister was now a ghost fish living in a pickle jar on my windowsill?

She came with me to buy baby carrots and loaves of stale bread from the one-dollar bin at Foodtown. She came with me to stand on the building's roof and realize you really could see stars in the city, despite what I'd been led to believe. I was anxious anytime we were apart, afraid the pickle jar on my windowsill would be empty when I got home, afraid that I'd imagined the entire thing: my sister, the fish, the waves. I took her everywhere except work, and even then, I hated that I had to leave her. At family meal, when the kitchen made dinner for the servers and front-of-house staff, I would sit alone, press my hand to my chest to remind myself of my sunburn from the day we went to the beach, push food around my plate. One night, I took a cab home that I couldn't afford because I couldn't handle another second of wondering whether or not she was a figment of my imagination. Noah, Jen, and the restaurant didn't matter, not now, not when something real was happening, and if she wasn't real, I wanted to live in the mirage as long as possible. I wanted to sit on my bed and talk to her. I dug my fingernails into the black seat as we stopped at another red light. The drive felt endless. When I got home, she was still there. She was always there. Over the next days, I experimented with reality. I tried closing my eyes hard and opening them. I tried staying up all night, watching her. I tried drinking most of a bottle of wine. But sober, drunk, two a.m., first thing in the morning, there she was.

❧

I was less anxious by my second Friday shift. Nothing takes away the new-girl jitters like a dead person reappearing as a ghost fish. But then I trudged up the stairs to the June and entered chaos. A server I hadn't met yet saw me as I walked in and said, "Oh, thank god you're here."

Though this didn't bode well, it still felt good to be recognized, then needed, in that order. He introduced himself—his name was Juan—and could I bus the tables outside that were full of empty wineglasses and dirty linen napkins?

I got to work quickly. The mood of the customers in the restaurant was irritable, bordering on rancid: folded arms, raised brows. After I cleared the empty tables, I started filling water glasses, seating new dinner guests as our next wave of reservations rolled in. My sister was in a pickle jar in my bedroom while I folded napkins. It was hard to take the irritable businessmen seriously, their arms crossed as they waited for their glasses of scotch.

It was almost ten by the time I was behind the host stand, taking my first breath of the evening. This was so different from my slow training shift and weeknight dinners; it was busy and fast and overwhelming. As I walked a party to their seats, a hotel guest who was trying to get to the bar stepped on my foot. When I looked at him, he scowled at me.

"Watch where you're going," he snapped as I limped back outside to my stack of menus.

Juan walked down the stairs, came to a halt beside me.

"Thanks for your help tonight," he said.

"Sure."

"Did you eat?" he asked.

"No, not yet. I missed family meal, I think."

"There's still food in the back. Nobody had time to eat, so Gabi ordered pizza."

"That's nice." I paused for a beat, flipping through the Rolodex in my head, trying to remember who I'd met so far that was nice enough to order everyone pizza. It wasn't the scary bartender with veiny forearms who hadn't spoken to me since my first training shift, even though we always worked together; that was Mike. Samuel was a busser and Juan was a server. "Who's Gabi?" I asked.

"Ah, right, you haven't met Gabrielle," he said. "I was surprised she hadn't sunk her teeth into the new girl yet."

Teeth. This felt ominous, like I was dessert.

"She was on vacation when you started," Juan continued. "She's a server most days but once a week she's the captain."

"Captain?" I asked, imagining a woman standing on the deck of a big ship, holding a spyglass to her eye.

"It means she's a manager who gets tipped out instead of salaried. So they can use her as a manager but don't have to give another person insurance, essentially." Juan put his hands in the pockets of the apron wound around his waist. "Brandon isn't here. He took today off."

I had wondered where Brandon was, was surprised I hadn't seen the glow of his shiny head or been micromanaged on menu placement that night. I was almost disappointed. Despite the chaos, it had been a decent shift, maybe one of my best yet.

"Good for him," I said.

Juan laughed. "Go eat. I'll watch the host stand." I felt less nervous than I had at prior family meals, where it had been hard not to feel like an interloper, sitting alone at a two-top in the back of the restaurant, scarfing down mystery lasagna while everyone else sat in booths and complained about the food before wiping the casserole dishes clean. Now I felt less like I was in everyone's way. Maybe having my sister back made everything else seem less important, or maybe I just finally felt useful and capable, but whatever the reason, the egg of anxiety inside of me had almost vanished.

The solarium was designed to look like a greenhouse, all fake frosted windows and leafy plants. My stomach grumbled. I had barely eaten since the night before. I entered the room quietly, like I was trying to slip into a pool without creating a ripple.

"It's you," someone said as I reached for a slice of pizza atop a teetering stack of grease-stained boxes. They were piled on a table that was candlelit, set for service, even though the dining room was rarely full enough to warrant seating in the solarium. Dinner plates, creamy white with gold rims, and heavy silverware on white tablecloths limned the scene. It was a still life of sorts, a strange one, and I pulled my hand back as I noticed a girl who looked familiar sitting in the back corner of the solarium.

I hadn't seen her when I walked in. It was the girl with the rings on her fingers that had sparkled like frost, the girl from my interview. She was at a table in the low light and I realized who she reminded me of, finally: She looked almost exactly like Lillian, Dillon's girlfriend from the bookstore in Awnor. Her dark hair was pulled back into a smooth, thick ponytail just like the day I saw her scratching a vase of flowers onto a server's pad of paper. She was sitting at a two-top with Mike the bartender. They were drinking from coffee mugs; their plates held the bones of leftover pizza.

"I'm Gabrielle," she said. I looked around to make sure she was speaking to me.

"You're the girl who came to the interview with the sequined Coach bag," she continued. "I used to have the same one when I was younger." For a second, I wondered if it *had* been her bag, Gabrielle's, that my sister found in a Goodwill bin all those years ago. But that was ridiculous. It was strange, the feeling I was having, that there was some kind of thread connecting me to this girl I didn't know.

"Alison," I said. "Nice to see you again." My hair was frizzy in its braid. I felt young and unkempt as I tugged at the end of it, a nervous habit I hated myself for having.

She laughed, but not in a mean way, I was almost sure.

"Welcome to the June," she said. "It's so lovely to have someone here to break up the monotony of this sausage fest."

The words *sausage fest* sounded strange coming out of her mouth. There was a lilt to her voice that I couldn't place. Like me, she spoke more slowly than people who'd grown up in the city, but she also had a tinge of some other accent, especially around her *o*'s.

"Thank you," I said.

"Eat," she replied, waving a hand toward the pizza.

"Who are you, again?" the bartender asked.

"Alison. The new host."

"What do you do, Alison?" Gabrielle asked from her seat. I noticed that their mugs were filled with red wine. I wanted some but did not ask.

"I work here?" I said. It felt like a trick question. She laughed again.

"But what do you *do*? Like, are you working on a film? Are you a sculptor? Writer?" Gabrielle asked. The edges of her lips quirked up again.

"Oh," I said. "Just this for now, I guess." I didn't say: *I'm being haunted by my dead sister who is now a fish, I'm avoiding my perfectly nice roommates, and I'm planning to continue hooking up with an attractive but probably disappointing guy.*

"I would have guessed she was a writer. Playwright," she said, looking at the bartender. He didn't comment.

I felt myself wanting to impress Gabrielle even though she had just referred to me in the third person, but I didn't know what to say. I put a slice of pizza on a plate, sat down, and looked at it as if it could give me some direction. My feet were tired. I picked up the slice and took a bite while trying not to stare at her. She was wearing a white T-shirt and black trousers, a normal outfit that somehow looked incredible on her. Her fingernails were unpainted, naked and shiny, and she had the elegant, thin hands of a pianist or, I imagined, an architect. She wore a gold necklace, a delicate chain that something round and coin-like dangled from. She had gone back to chatting with the bartender and fiddled with the chain where it hung at her chest. I tried not to watch, tried to unglue my eyes from her fingers, the chain. I felt like my gaze was heavy on her, like something impossible not to feel. But what? It was just my eyes, just her hands.

I picked a pepperoni off my pizza, wiped the grease from my fingers on a linen napkin. There was something ironic about how often I now used linen napkins and ate from nice, heavy plates by candlelight. None of these shiny things were mine, but here I was nonetheless, existing inside of this pretty picture. I couldn't afford to eat at a place like this, except I ate here more nights than I didn't.

"I'm sorry I haven't had the chance to welcome you yet," Gabrielle said when I stood up to put my empty plate in the bus bin and return to my post outside. I had no idea whether or not she was being sarcastic. She didn't seem like the kind of person who would say something so earnest.

"That's okay," I said. My voice came out almost in a squeak and I felt embarrassed.

"I've been controlling the chaos tonight," she said. "A pipe burst downstairs in the kitchen, if you can believe it. And I was away for a bit for the summer."

Mike laughed.

"That's what Gabi *does*," he said. "She goes on vacation." He said something in Spanish that made Gabrielle laugh. She responded with a smack on his shoulder and I wondered if they were together.

"Have another slice if you want," Gabrielle said. I hadn't realized she was still looking at me. Something about the weight of her full attention was overwhelming.

"I'm okay," I said. "Juan is watching the host stand, so."

"Okay." Gabrielle shrugged.

"Thanks for the pizza," I said.

"Of course. I'm really glad you're here."

It was a nice thing for her to say, *I'm really glad you're here.* I wasn't sure if she meant it and I didn't know how to respond to such frank niceness, so I just said something like *Okay, thanks*, dropped my plate in a bus bin, and returned to the host stand. I wanted to hear her say those words again: *I'm really glad you're here.* But how could she be glad? What did she know about me? I didn't really know anything about myself. *I* didn't know if I was glad that I was there.

"Did you eat already? That was fast," Juan said.

"Was it? It felt like I was gone forever."

He laughed. "I guess you met Gabrielle, then," he said as he turned and walked back inside.

"How are you?" I asked a couple as they approached the host stand, looking for a table for two. "I'm really glad you're here," I said as they followed me into the restaurant, trying the words out in my mouth.

It was five after midnight, the end of my shift, and I was desperate to run home and check on my sister, but I didn't know the rules of the restaurant with Gabrielle in charge, whether I could just clock out or if I needed to check with her first. Brandon usually told me when I could go home but I'd barely seen Gabrielle all evening, and I was sure that I would rather stand on the sidewalk all night than ask her a childish question like *May I please go home now?*

I stood indecisively behind the host stand, stacking and restacking the menus in an effort to look busy. There was nobody sitting at the tables outside, no real reason for me to still be clocked in. People walked past me toward the West Village and I bit the tip of my nail on my right thumb and peeled it off with my teeth. I hadn't bitten my nails since middle school. I felt like I was growing backward, back to sleeping in a twin bed, back to having hopeless crushes and feeling nervous almost all the time, back to when I was sixteen and a bartender named Angel at the restaurant where I worked wrapped her thin hands around my hips to move me out of her way one busy night. It made my heart beat in my throat, the way she touched me. I was losing years; I was blushing constantly; I was happy just to be there, and my sister was alive.

I was still shuffling the menus on the host stand when I glanced over my shoulder at the front door. Gabrielle was standing on the bottom step, right behind me, and I jumped.

"Oh my god, you scared me. I didn't see you come out," I said.

She stepped onto the sidewalk and stood next to me. Our shoulders brushed and her skin felt warm, like she'd been standing in the sun.

"Why are you still here?" Gabrielle asked.

I shrugged.

"My mother used to do that. When you're thinking or when you don't know the answer to a question, you shrug and you stick your bottom lip out. Like a little pout. Very French."

"I do not." I sounded standoffish, but secretly I was pleased she'd noticed something about me. I wondered if her mother was French. It seemed intoxicatingly interesting, a French mother.

"How long have you lived here?" I asked.

"Mmm, a couple of years, I guess," she replied.

"What do you do?" I asked, hoping it didn't sound like a snide reference to her earlier question. I was genuinely curious.

"I'm an artist. Painter. Oils, mostly. Some photography." She shrugged. "I dreamed of an Alice Neel existence, but alas," she said, waving a hand around as if to display her kingdom.

The ring on her middle finger was a jagged emerald that glinted as it caught the light spilling out of the lobby. I had a million questions, more than that. I nodded as if I understood and could relate, as if I knew who Alice Neel was—as if, as if, as if.

"You can go home whenever, you know. I'm not like Brandon, I don't give a fuck, obviously." She laughed, a short bark. I could tell she was wrestling with the power of being a manager or captain or whatever she was, wanting to be the cool person in charge who bought us pizza and let us run amok instead of lecturing us about roll-ups like Brandon. But I wanted to be her equal. I wanted to be significant enough that Gabrielle *did* give a fuck, actually.

"Okay" was all I could actually think to say.

"I'll see you tomorrow," she replied.

I checked my phone as I walked home. Noah had texted me—*wya*—around nine and what I assumed was a drunken *hello????* around eleven.

Hi, sorry, can't hang out my sister is in town, I typed. Then I deleted the words and put my phone back in my bag without responding.

When I opened my bedroom door, my sister's fins waved from the jar. I exhaled. The Golden Girls were laughing from the screen of my laptop. It had become a habit to leave a movie or show playing for my sister whenever I had to go out.

Betty White took something out of the oven. I fell face-first onto my bed, dramatically, then rolled over onto my back, crossed my arms over my chest. I craned my neck over the pillow, looking at her jar upside down. It didn't matter if I was the only person in the world who knew, definitively, that ghosts were real. It didn't matter, because I was watching a television show with my sister in my apartment in New York. The most mundane thing in the world was magic.

"I'm so happy," I said out loud to my sister. It was such a simple sentence, so earnest, and I didn't care. I was happy, so happy I felt like I might cry.

I turned the laptop so we could both see. Rose was laughing in a convertible. I tried a laugh too. I was laughing with my sister in my apartment in New York. I felt a little glow in me, something like warmth.

I set my alarm so I didn't accidentally sleep until noon. I wanted my sister to see more of the city than the grocery store and my apartment building. *I* wanted more. When I woke up, I put on a black skirt and a black top and put her in the *thank you thank you thank you* tote bag so I could feel her jar bump against my hip as we went down the stairs in my apartment. For a moment, she was bumping her human hip against mine, we were girls walking toward the beach on a hot summer afternoon and I wasn't paying attention to what she was saying. "Earth to Alison," she said. She would have said.

We stepped out of the apartment. A tow truck pulled up in front of our building, then curtsied back toward a red car, loudly beeping. Its hard metal cross unfolded toward its target. At home, tow trucks were for cars that got stuck in flooded streets during hurricane season, like our mom's green Ford so many years ago. There weren't enough people, or maybe there wasn't enough money for tow trucks, for anyone to care how long a car was left parked somewhere. We watched the truck disappear down Avenue A with the car strapped to its back. Things could be taken so quickly. Things were taken so quickly, while people slept in their beds.

We walked through Tompkins Square Park, where a trio of women who looked grandmother-age were playing jazz. I sat on a bench and put my sister's jar beside me so she could watch.

What I really wanted to understand were the rules of her existence. I wanted to know that I could keep her forever. I wanted to know that she would never disappear from me again. Once more, I wondered if I was the only one who could see her. I looked around, checking faces for flickers of recognition, of awe, at this fish that was bobbing up and down in a pickle jar, keeping time to the music, but nobody so much as glanced at us. But she was so real, so solid it seemed impossible that she might be invisible to everyone else. Then again, a fish in a jar wasn't the strangest thing to see in a city park. I thought about asking someone to tell me what color she was so I could stop wondering, so I could settle the fact of her existence. But she was watching the woman playing the trombone with something like fascination in her sister-ghost-fish eyes. She was so completely my sister. Her scales were glowing. She was real. She couldn't have been more real.

The women began a song about waiting for someone to come home. We sat and watched, my sister's fins waving lazily back and forth, and I knew then that she, that this, was only for us. It didn't matter that no one else could see her, my sister, existing alongside me. It started to rain lightly, a warm summer drizzle we could barely feel through the branches of the tree we sat beneath, and for just a moment, a rainbow appeared. I picked up my sister's jar and held it as gently as I could.

Good luck, I mouthed to her, pointing her in the direction of the sun shower, rain dripping through the rainbow. She bobbed up and down, as if saying *Yes, it is, a rainbow above a trio of musicians in a park in a city must mean something. It must mean something good.* I pulled my phone out of my bag and googled Alice Neel. She painted bright, intense portraits of people she loved and people she didn't even know. I wondered what it was like, to be so unafraid of other people like that.

As the musicians packed up their instruments, I checked the time on my phone. I wondered if Gabrielle was on the schedule. I was still new enough that I hadn't yet memorized everyone's normal shifts.

"Do you want to come to work with me?" I asked my sister.

It felt cruel to leave her alone at home yet again. She was bobbing her head but I couldn't tell if it meant *yes* or *no.* I put her back in the bag and walked carefully down St. Marks, not wanting anyone to jostle her. One night at work wouldn't hurt.

I regretted bringing my sister almost as soon as I arrived. I hung my bag on the hook in the hutch and realized how long a drop it was to the floor if someone accidentally bumped into her. I imagined the bag on the ground, broken glass, a pool of water, and my sister gone. There was a cabinet beneath the POS system, the computer we used to punch in orders and print checks. I opened it: empty. I stuffed the tote bag in there. The wooden cabinet was warped and the doors didn't close neatly. I had to slam them shut. This no longer seemed like a good idea.

"Sorry," I whispered to the cabinet, hoping my sister could hear me. I looked around. If Mike, the bartender who was friends with Gabrielle, saw me talking to a cabinet, I'd have to quit this job and find a new one.

The night dragged on and on. There was a total of two reservations, and I kept picking up empty glasses and handing out too many menus, any excuse to return to the hutch and check on my sister. She did not look happy. In the dark of the hutch, her scales looked dull, and my stomach flipped. I had the urge to pull out my phone, as if her fading color were a symptom I could google and then fix. Gabrielle wasn't working that night. I'd felt momentarily disappointed and then relieved. I could feel myself moving stiffly, my motions stilted, as if I were being recorded.

To distract myself, I stood at the bar and helped roll forks and knives into their blue-and-white-striped napkins. I liked making a stack, a pyramid of silverware, that Mike would silently slide off the bar and pass to the busboy.

I stood there and rolled and wondered who'd chosen the music for the lobby and restaurant. It was piped-in classical, pieces that felt either lazy and slow or too frenetic, violins screeching. It made me think of my grandmother sitting for hours in the kitchen, listening to plastic cassette tapes of people playing delicate instruments. Once, my sister and I had shown her a YouTube video on my school-issued laptop of the Royal Concertgebouw Orchestra in Amsterdam playing *La Mer*. We thought she would be excited to see the music played by real people, but when the video ended, I looked over and she was crying. She told us never to show her anything like that again. Classical music always made me feel sad for my grandmother, alone in the kitchen.

Around nine, Brandon walked out to the host stand and raised his eyebrows at me. I was fanning myself with the wine list but put it down when I saw the look on his face. I was hot, sweat beading on my forehead, from running in and out of the restaurant all night.

"It's dead. You can go early if you want," he said.

"I want!" I said. My voice came out louder than I'd meant it to. I didn't really want to clock out early, shorten my paycheck, but I was desperate to get my sister out of the cabinet and take her home.

"Jesus, don't act too excited," he said. "See you tomorrow."

"You'll be here? But isn't tomorrow Gabrielle's day?" I asked. I couldn't help myself. "To be captain, I mean."

"Whatever, the day after. You're very literal," Brandon said.

I retrieved my sister from the cabinet, then went down the kitchen stairs to clock out and exited from the service staircase. As soon as I was out of the restaurant, standing on the corner of Eighth and Fifth, I took my sister out of my bag. Her water looked a little cloudy and her scales were definitely duller. Or were they? I couldn't tell for sure. Maybe they just seemed duller because it was dark.

She floated near the bottom of the jar. I squinted at her beneath the streetlight. Were her scales less glittery than they had been before, in the daytime? It was almost imperceptible, maybe even just a symptom of my anxious mind, but I wished there were someone I could ask: Does this fish look less bright to you? When I thought about it too hard, an hourglass flipped in my stomach, sand racing downward.

"Sorry," I whispered to her. "We're going home now."

She waved a fin weakly as if to say, *Don't worry about it.* I was worried.

"Alison?" I heard a familiar voice say. I shoved the jar back into my bag and turned around.

"Oh, hey, Mai," I said.

"Hey." She looked past me. "Who are you talking to?"

"Oh, I was just, um, on the phone." I pulled my phone out of my back pocket as if it were evidence. "Bad connection, though."

"Oh. Yeah. Probably hard to talk on the phone if it's in your pocket."

"Ha," I replied flatly. "What are you up to?"

"Just stopping by to say hey to Samuel. I think he's getting cut early, though."

"Yeah, it was slow," I said. We looked at each other for an awkward beat. I wondered if she believed me or if she thought I was insane. Possibly both.

"Okay, well. Bye," Mai said.

I waved goodbye as she disappeared down the sidewalk toward the June. I could almost hear my sister laughing at the absurdity of it all.

❧

I'd forgotten how easy it was to exist around people who knew me, people I didn't have to tiptoe around or bring menus and water to or be *bright-bright-bright!* so they would want to be my friend. With my sister on the windowsill, I talked and talked. I asked her questions. She couldn't respond, but it didn't matter. It felt so good to speak.

I was trying to remember every single day she had missed in chronological order, from the first day without her to the first day with her, and describe them, all the days that stacked on top of each other, so it would be like she had never been gone at all. Now she knew about Dillon and Lillian and our grandmother passing away on the day of my high-school graduation. I was surprised to find that I could almost laugh about it all with her, everything that had gone wrong since I'd lost her. The miserable, unbelievable irony was ours to share and it was a relief to have someone who understood it all exactly.

I still didn't understand what had brought her back to me, my sister-ghost-fish, but I knew I had to be so careful with her. I didn't want to disturb whatever was happening. If I was quiet, if I was good, if I didn't ask too many questions, maybe I could keep this haunting, keep her.

The only thing I hadn't mentioned yet was Gabrielle. Not that there was anything to tell, except that she was stuck in my head like a song that everyone loved, every radio played. I had an instinct, though, to keep her to myself.

One Saturday night when I wasn't working, I took my sister out on the fire escape. My feet were bare and the bottoms were black from the dirty grate. I felt like a wild thing in my denim cutoffs and white tank, my shoulders brown from the sun. I felt beautiful. Did she feel beautiful too? Her scales almost glowed in the rusty light of the summer dusk.

"Look at us," I said. "We live in New York." She bobbed in her jar. Her fish mouth flickered toward a smile.

That night, stretched out on my bed, watching another episode of *Golden Girls* on my laptop, I smelled popcorn being popped in the microwave, heard the low laugh of Leo or Marcus, I wasn't sure which. I glanced at my sister and her eyes were closed, her fins still. Despite myself, I wondered if she would ever be able to talk back to me or if I would spend the rest of my twenties in this room, chattering away to a girl who was a ghost in the shape of a fish. I rolled onto my side, curled myself into a comma, and felt guilty for the thought. All I had wanted since her death was her, and here she was. How could I ask for more? What more could I possibly need?

⁓

Sunday morning was brunch, universally regarded as the most dreaded shift for anyone who has ever worked in a restaurant. I spotted Gabrielle before I even crossed Fifth Avenue. I knew it was her; I could tell from the way she weaved through the tables like a dancer on opening night, somehow deliberate and graceful even with an armful of roll-ups, setting the stage. I waved as I got closer.

"Morning," I said.

She nodded in reply. There were purple circles below her eyes. I wondered if she'd gone out the night before. Since my sister's arrival I hadn't attended any Bushwick house parties or danced in a purple-painted club. I hadn't texted Noah or heard from Jen. I had been quiet and protective and good. I was a big sister again. I would not wonder if I was missing out on anything. I would not wish for more.

Mai and Samuel, a busser I'd worked only a couple of shifts with so far, stood in the hutch. Mai was wearing the server's uniform, a white button-down, black pants, and a blue apron. I was surprised—Mai was supposed to be a host like me.

"Good morning," I said.

"Morning," Samuel replied.

"Hey," Mai said flatly.

They both had tired, heavy eyes that matched Gabrielle's and were clutching cups filled with espresso with both hands.

"Promotion?" I asked Mai as I slid by her to hang my bag on the hook.

"I guess," she replied. I felt a slight twinge of jealousy that she'd be receiving tips now. I took a deep breath and retreated back outside. There were no reservations scribbled in the leather-bound book, but it was a nice morning and the air felt cool and clean. I stood behind the host stand with my back straight.

First came the hotel guests, bleary-eyed and half dressed, looking for coffee. Then came the neighborhood regulars, less bleary-eyed, impatient for their usual tables. Next were the tourists and they came in waves, and before ten, I had a list of twelve parties waiting for tables. We didn't take online reservations or hand out pagers to alert waiting guests that a table was ready, so if people wanted to eat, they had to stand on the sidewalk outside the hotel until there was a place to seat them. The problem was that this created an obstacle course for the servers and the busboys to weave through, and the servers and busboys were already in bad moods on warm Sunday mornings.

Brandon appeared and hissed, "You've got to get these people off the sidewalk." His breath was hot and acidic, like coffee. I started to sweat. I didn't know how to do that. They all wanted to sit outside and they all said they'd rather wait than be seated in the restaurant inside with plenty of tables and air-conditioning.

Gabrielle walked up to the host stand and stood behind me, her eyes wide and bright now.

"Who's first?" she asked, looking at my scribbled list of people waiting for tables.

"The Jacksons, it's a three-top," I said, pointing to a kid about our age in khaki pants and loafers next to two people who looked like his parents, their hair matching shades of gray, both wearing hiking shoes and purple NYU T-shirts. She glanced over, then fixed me with her sea-glass stare.

"You're the host. You're in charge. There's a three-top in the solarium; tell them they'll be sitting there. Don't ask. Tell."

I wasn't sure if she was annoyed or just giving me advice, but it worked. They followed me inside to the solarium, and the next handful of parties did as well. Soon, there was only one group left waiting, small enough that they could wait on the black metal benches flanking the hotel's entrance. I stood behind the host stand and organized the menus the servers unceremoniously dumped there, wiping off the ones with bits of poached egg or tomato sauce.

When Gabrielle returned to check on her tables outside, I said, "Thank you. Sorry. That was a mess."

She shook her head. "Don't ever apologize here. There is zero training, and nothing makes sense even if there were. It's all backward. The owner wants this place to be the hotel version of a Wes Anderson film. I mean, using this thing instead of online reservations like every other restaurant?" She gestured toward the leather reservations book. "Absurd."

I liked the way she pronounced every syllable. Everything she did seemed decisive. I was relieved that she wasn't annoyed at me. Or at least not visibly annoyed.

"Go take a break. There's coffee behind the café bar in the lobby for staff," she said.

"Thanks."

I went inside but skipped the coffee, though I was grateful that she was imparting some of the staff secrets. I stood in the hutch, in the corner that bent back from the door like a pocket or a mouse's burrow. I dug my phone out of my bag and sat on a milk crate flipped upside down in the corner. I could feel a headache creeping up on me, the back of my skull dully throbbing. I felt strange in my body, perched on the plastic crate, trying not to fuck anything else up. Being around Gabrielle reminded me that I lived in a city where I could tell strangers what to do and, like magic, they would listen. I felt torn between the desire to go home and check on my sister and the quiet longing to be out in the city, surrounding myself with other people, the moment I was cut from my shift.

Hey Jen, are you doing anything tn?

I let the cursor *blink, blink, blink.* What I really wanted was to ask Gabrielle what she was doing after work. I hit Send anyway and stared at the screen for a long minute before returning my phone to my bag and going outside to find the Kellys, party of four, a table where they could eat avocado toast and eighteen-dollar oatmeal.

I didn't look at my phone again until I was clocking out, a process that was about as technologically advanced as the reservation system and involved writing down my name and the number of hours that I'd worked in a binder, crossing my fingers that whoever did payroll would be able to read my scrawl. Jen hadn't responded to my text but she'd posted pictures on her social media account.

I tossed my phone in my bag. I felt a wave of aloneness, of being unmoored from all of the real-life people existing with other real-life people. But I felt like I had a Ping-Pong ball in my throat because I wasn't alone, I had my sister, my ghost, my fish, in a jar on my windowsill at home.

I went to the staff bathroom, a room in the bowels of the hotel that was tiled in a sick, pale green and always smelled moist, like damp earth. My face was shiny and there was something sticky on the hem of my shirt. Honey. I looked in the mirror: My cheeks were flushed from being outside all morning and my eyes looked tired. I put a hand to my face, my fingers to my lips. I could feel myself, the soft skin of my cheek against the pads of my fingers, but the image in the mirror felt like someone far away. I dropped my hands and left via the service staircase so I didn't have to say goodbye to anyone. I felt like if I saw Gabrielle again today, I would want to change my life, cut my hair, get on an airplane, learn a new language. Something about her, the way she moved and spoke, how sure of herself she was, confused everything I thought I knew. Her decisiveness, her ability to speak French and Spanish with a perfect accent, the way she said, "I'm an artist," her smooth ponytail, all of it made me feel like there was something sour on my tongue. I didn't know which I wanted more, to be her or to know her.

When I reached the top of the staircase and pushed the door open onto Eighth Street, I felt restless. I decided to walk toward the water. My body was so tired that I didn't even have the energy to feel guilty for not going home, not checking on my sister whose pickle-jar water, I was now convinced, was becoming cloudier by the day. It took every drop of my mental energy to force one foot in front of the other, which felt good. An exercise in endurance.

I walked five blocks, then five more, crossed a busy road, and stood on a walkway above the water. As far back as I could remember, I'd do this dumb thing where I promised myself I would change after just one more decisive action. A haircut or a long drive would be the thing that finally morphed me into the beautiful, brilliant girl I was supposed to be. It hadn't worked yet but maybe this, this walk, this view, would be it. After this walk, after I got home, I would finally be a better person. I would show up early to work. I would take tender care of my sister-ghost-fish. I would not see Noah again. I would get a library card.

I wasn't sure where I was, exactly, but it smelled briny, like home, the ocean that gives and gives and takes and takes. I could hear the water lapping against the earth. It didn't sound dangerous, but I felt lightheaded where I stood, suspended over it by a metal sheet. People said that Manhattan was an island, but the sandy, empty town where I used to live felt more like one than where I stood now. The thought of the Atlantic Ocean—stretching all the way from where I came to where I was—made me almost homesick. I thought about my sister, the invisible thread that I could feel no matter where I went. I thought it had been severed when she drowned, but I felt it again now, tugging me toward her.

I couldn't remember which way my apartment was, so I walked a few blocks, got on a bus that was going east, and sat down in one of the gray plastic seats toward the back. My sister, the smell of salt in the air, my head, Gabrielle weaving like a ribbon through the outdoor tables, Noah, the Atlantic Ocean reaching home, it all turned into tears that leaked down my face and onto the collar of my shirt. I was soaked in salt and honey and I wanted to start over, already, again.

Sunday was my last day of work for the week. I slept until nine, then lay in bed until ten, when I heard the rest of my room-mates wake up, rustle around, and leave for work or whatever they did on Mondays. My sister was in the jar on the window-sill above my head. I scooted her over so she wasn't stuck in the direct beam of the hot sun. I got out of bed to make a cup of instant coffee in the kitchen, drank the coffee, took three Advils, and fell back asleep. When I woke up again, it was afternoon. My room was hot. My head still hurt, and I wasn't any different at all.

I retrieved my phone from the bag I'd dropped in the corner of my room the night before. My bones and my eyes felt heavy. I lay on my side, curled like a cupped hand. My sister's scales looked less vivid than I remembered them being the day before. In my half-awake state I wondered if my bad mood or depression or whatever was contagious. I realized I hadn't showered since before I'd gone to work, so I crawled out of bed, dragged myself to the bathroom, and turned the water on as hot as it could go. I opened the door after I was done and watched the steam roll out into the hall.

"Are you okay?" I asked my sister later, back in my room. She looked so gentle in the dark blue light.

She looked at me. I should have felt guilty for neglecting her all day, but all I could feel was a knot of grief in my stomach. I rolled over and closed my eyes.

I had forgotten what it was like to feel responsible for a person you loved more than your own beating heart. My sister on my windowsill was such a comfort. I loved my constant shadow. I could almost feel her fingers behind some curtain, brushing my shoulders. But I felt something cobwebby at the corners of myself—resentment, or guilt. Her scales were less orange than when she'd first appeared, and like the summer she'd died, I didn't know how to help her.

At the same time, my sister lay beside me and rubbed my back until I fell asleep. Her water seeped into my sheets, and it was better than being alone. It was a dream.

Wasn't it?

I was surprised when Brandon scheduled me to help work a private event. It was a small reception for an author whose second book of essays had just been published. She was doing a reading at a bookstore nearby and her publisher had planned a small party for her afterward. It turned out the author used to be a manager at the June. When she arrived after her reading, a small bouquet of pink calla lilies in her arms, she kissed Mike on the cheek and asked to borrow his vape. He smiled warmly at her. Juan gave her a big hug, like she was an old friend returning home. I felt my fingertips tingling at the possibility of this, a woman who had likely stood near the host stand, where I stood for an infinity every night, now publishing books.

I was stationed near Gabrielle at the edge of the room. Servers passed around tiny trays of food and tall glasses of prosecco. The party guests were all well dressed and had beautiful skin.

"What was she like?" I asked Gabrielle.

"Who? The author?" Gabrielle asked.

"Yeah. I've never heard you guys talk about her before," I replied.

"Hm," Gabrielle said, a thinking noise that sounded like a hum in the back of her throat. "She was quiet," Gabrielle said finally. "Quiet and fun."

I didn't know those two traits could coexist. My fingers kept tingling. There wasn't much for me to do besides stand on the fringe next to Gabrielle. My only real assignment was to point party guests to the bathroom and make sure hotel guests knew that the restaurant was closed for an event—we're so sorry—but they were more than welcome to order from the bar. The author's beautiful girlfriend arrived, wrapped her arms around the author, kissed her on the lips, then pulled back and wiped something from the edge of her mouth, an errant flash of lip gloss. She leaned in, whispered something in the author's ear that made her eyes glitter. My cheeks burned. I tried not to look at Gabrielle. I felt like the most insignificant, unsophisticated living person in New York. I was, objectively, the most insignificant, unsophisticated person at that party. I didn't know anything. My cheeks were still burning. The truth was, I wasn't sure I had ever seen a woman kiss another woman in real life before. How was that possible? I felt like the end of a frayed electrical cord.

Gabrielle's fingers brushed my shoulder.

"Are you okay?" she asked. "You're...no offense, but you're sort of sweating. Glowing, even, but you're definitely hot. Do you need to sit down?"

I shook my head no. Then I said yes, actually, I did need to sit down for a second.

༄

When I walked into the hutch the next day, the restaurant was back to normal. No partygoers or authors draped in lilies. I hung my bag in my usual spot. Gabrielle was there, holding a coffee cup. Her face was twisted like she smelled something bad but was trying not to. Mike was bartending and had half his body stuck through the pass in an effort to suck on his lime-green vape without Brandon seeing him. I felt a pang of what-have-I-missed.

"Hey," I said.

"Fuck, this is not good," Gabrielle said, waving her cup. "Do you want the rest?"

When she said *fuck,* it sounded short and sharp, like a pebble in a shoe.

I took the coffee cup from her hands and sipped. It was room-temperature vodka, and I felt my face twist into an expression that matched hers. We looked at each other and laughed. I poured the rest of it down my throat and watched Gabrielle try not to smile in my direction. I liked surprising her. I could tell she liked being surprised.

She took the cup back and handed me a little plate with half a croissant on it. "You should have this. You look like you haven't slept."

I took a bite. It was warm and flaky and a tiny bit sweet. It was the best thing I had ever put in my mouth.

"Do I make you nervous?" she asked.

"A little," I said.

She was wearing rings on four of her ten fingers. She reached up with her pointer finger, wrapped in a gold snake, and wiped a crumb from my bottom lip. I crossed my arms, not wanting her to see how her finger on my lip made the hair on my arms stand up straight.

"I like you," she said. She slid by me in the narrow hutch and went back to prepping for dinner service without waiting to hear if I liked her too. I went downstairs to get the reservation book. I stood on the sidewalk and touched my lip where the crumb had been. I felt like I was imagining half of my life into existence.

On the stupid scale that Brandon had invented to describe the restaurant's business in his end-of-day logs—*mild, medium,* and *spicy*—the previous Sunday's brunch had been extra-spicy. This Thursday was blissfully mild. We had a few regulars, a few hotel guests who looked exhausted from walking around the city all day, a few first dates. Those were my favorites, the first dates. I always tried to seat them at tables close to the host stand so I could eavesdrop. The majority were, of course, bad: boys flashing money, girls whose faces fell when they spotted dates who did not match their online photos, people who just didn't find each other interesting, throwing out topics like wayward darts. But there was the sweet minority that was awkward but tender, two people sitting down for a slightly nerve-racking drink, expecting another mediocre evening and finding instead a lovely surprise.

Gabrielle's section was inside the restaurant that night, so I didn't see her much. Juan's section was the lobby and all of the tables outside, and Mike, as usual, was bartending. I liked when Juan had the outside tables. He had a good sense of humor and I never saw him get ruffled or annoyed. I had worked at the June for over a month now and his guests never left less than happy, even the snippiest ones. He didn't spend a lot of time on his tables but was warm and efficient. He came out around ten thirty as the last guests were ordering dessert.

"Gabi is looking for you," he said as he walked by me, rapping his knuckles on the host stand.

Gabrielle was looking for me. I couldn't quite figure out why she kept being nice to me. It seemed like she had enough friends, enough to do with her painting and long vacations. I cleared some wineglasses from an empty table, an excuse to leave the host stand and go inside. Gabrielle was at the end of the bar talking to Mike.

"Don't go home when Brandon cuts you," Gabrielle said.

I dropped a glass with a dark purple lipstick stain on it into the bus bin under the bar and it landed with a clear, high sound, the ring of a church bell.

"Okay," I said.

"Wait in the solarium. I'll come get you when it's time for family."

"Didn't we already have family? I remember tacos."

"It's after-hours family," Gabrielle replied. "Dessert."

After-hours family was at the bar. It was Mike, Gabrielle, Juan, Samuel, Mai, two of the line cooks from the kitchen downstairs, and me. There was leftover pasta, plates of it, and all the half-empty bottles of wine we served by the glass that hadn't been finished. I wondered if my sister would prefer a wine bottle to a pickle jar. Probably not. A devastating, almost morbidly funny image stuck in my head: her sister-ghost-fish body trapped midway down the neck of the bottle.

"What do you want to drink, West Virginia?" Mike asked me.

"I'm actually from—" I stopped. "Can I have a glass of wine?"

"Help yourself," he said, gesturing to the bottles on the bar. He put a clean glass in front of me.

"Just wine?" Gabrielle said, wrinkling her nose. "Can I have an old-fashioned, Mikey?"

"Bitch, I already cleaned the sink."

"The a.m. shift won't care. They never finish setup for us." Mike rolled his eyes, but he made her what she wanted.

Mai was looking at something on Samuel's phone, laughing. Juan was nursing a glass of whiskey poured over one giant ice cube. Mike was talking in a low voice into his phone, facing the wineglasses hung upside down in metal racks on the wall of the bar, his back toward us. My hands needed something to do. I poured wine into my glass.

"So we're going to Grace's next?" Gabrielle said. She asked most questions as if she knew the answer already.

Mike turned abruptly. "Yes," he said to us, then "Grace's," to whoever he was whispering to on the other end of the line.

"Nooo, Gabi." Juan groaned. He had a hand, clean and strong, wrapped around the base of his glass. "You are going to kill us, chiquita."

Gabrielle smiled. "Alison hasn't been yet. Alison just moved here."

"Alison," Juan said, "I can assure you that there is more to this wonderful city than Grace's. You look like a smart girl. We should go to bed, wake up, and enjoy tomorrow, right?"

"I just moved here, I've never been," I said. I winked at him, surprising myself, and he laughed. Out of the corner of my eye, I clocked Gabrielle smiling too.

"Alison! I thought we were on similar pages. Fine, we'll go to Grace's. But just for one, yes?"

I nodded and tried not to grin too widely, delighted at finally being included in their secret club. I couldn't wait to tell my sister. I finished my wine and poured more from a different bottle. It was bubbly this time, a sharp carbonation I could feel in my nose that made me want to laugh a little bit. I listened as Juan and Mike talked about a new cocktail that was going on the fall menu. Juan spoke with a cadence, a rhythm, like a lullaby. He was probably the most aloof, private person who worked at the restaurant. He never had sex with someone in the walk-in or broke things, he never told little lies to get out of a shift, never even stole toilet paper from the storage closet downstairs. He had kids, a house in Queens, a life he'd made out of shifts at this restaurant. He kept the tarnished edges of the June polished. He was kind and had our respect in a way nobody else did, not even Brandon or Chef.

We put our glasses in bus bins, recycled the empty bottles. Mike wiped down the bar one last time and we walked down the kitchen stairs to the service exit. The kitchen was off-limits to hosts and I felt a little swell of excitement, seeing it enormous in the dark. It looked strange without noise or light, sterile in its emptiness.

Grace's was two blocks from the June. I walked by it almost every day but never so much as glanced inside. It was one of those places that you walked down a few stairs to enter, and it was cave-like and busy even on a Thursday night.

Gabrielle grabbed my hand and pulled me with her to the bar. Her palm was sweaty against mine. I'd expected her skin to be cool to the touch, but her slick grip reminded me she was a human being with a hot beating heart, just like mine. She squeezed before she let go.

"Gabi," the bartender said, nodding to her.

"Hey, Jake," Gabrielle said, her tone terse, but I saw her shoulders roll back, her spine elongate. They had almost certainly hooked up before.

"What can I get you?" he asked.

"Two tequila sodas," Gabrielle said. "Espolòn."

"Sure," he said. "Who's your friend?"

I gave an awkward wave. "I'm Ali," I said, then corrected myself: "Alison."

To the people at home, most of whom I'd known all my life, I was Ali. I wanted the entirety of my name here, for a change.

"Hello, Ali-Alison," he said, and put out his hand for me to shake. I couldn't tell if he was mocking me or not with the formal gesture, but I took his hand and gave it a hard squeeze.

Grace's was a narrow space with a bar that ran down the entire length of the left side. The rest of the room was filled with high-top tables, all wooden and splintery. We sat at one with our drinks.

"So," Gabrielle said after she'd taken a sip. "How's New York so far? Where do you live?"

I wanted to say every word exactly right. I felt my shoulders roll back, spine elongate, mirroring hers.

"Alphabet City," I replied. "What about you?"

She laughed. "I've never heard anyone but a real estate agent use that term. I live in the East Village too. Across the street from Tompkins."

"Wow," I said. "I live in, like, a prison cell on Avenue D."

"Do you know anyone who lives in the city?" she asked.

I pictured my sister on my windowsill, alone.

"No. I mean, yeah. A girl named Jen who I went to high school with lives near me. I've seen her a few times." I couldn't mention my sister and the pickle jar, obviously. I cleared my throat. "And I know some of her friends, I guess."

"Dating anyone?"

"No. Not really," I said, trying not to visualize the painting of horses on Noah's wall.

"I don't recommend it," she said. "New York boys are infamously resistant to becoming anything other than boys."

"So you don't date?" I asked. Gabrielle laughed.

"What made you move here?" she asked, ignoring my question.

"I was bored," I said flatly. It felt like a good answer to give Gabrielle, the artist.

"Bored," she repeated, looking at me straight on. "Hmm. Finish your drink," she said and she stood up and walked back to the bar.

I was learning that Gabrielle was direct. She was domineering but without arrogance, for the most part. She didn't need it. There was something precise about her, like her entire existence was a hyper-realistic painting. I could still feel her hot hand in mine. I finished my drink.

Juan slid into the seat across from me, replacing Gabrielle.

"Shots," he said, putting down two paper cups that looked like the ones cheap motels put on bathroom counters for mouthwash. We cheers'd, threw them back. Tequila dribbled down my chin.

"Ugh." I grimaced. I felt a little drunk. I wondered if my sister was worried about me. I hadn't stayed out this late since she'd reappeared. I checked my phone to see what time it was and felt a twinge of guilt.

"What happened to just one?" I teased Juan.

He smiled. I looked down at my fingers, which were fiddling with my empty shot glass. I had a bad habit of picking at my cuticles, and my ragged hands embarrassed me. I put them under the table, in my lap. I tried not to look past him at Gabrielle, who was still standing at the bar talking to the bartender, Jake. She folded her arms over her chest and shook her head at him, but I could tell she was holding back a smile.

"Should we do another?" I asked.

"Oh, no. That's enough for me," he said, then surprised me by kissing me on both cheeks. "Ciao, ciao, see you tomorrow."

"Thanks for the shot," I said.

He waved to Gabrielle and was gone. I wanted to go too. I wanted to watch TV with my sister and think about nothing. I pulled my phone out of my bag. Gabrielle was leaning close to Jake. I felt a flash of something, something close to jealousy. Gabrielle finally returned with beers, more shots, and Mike, who sat on the stool next to me. The bar was packed now and filled with a comforting, mind-numbing buzz. A girl with a gold hoop in her septum slid onto the stool next to Gabrielle, across from us.

"Did you guys hear about Laurel Place? It fucking caught on fire during dinner service," she said, laughing. "Can you imagine?"

"That's crazy karma, dude." Mike laughed and said something else about a restaurant he had apparently worked at for a short time. He was drunk and his face looked looser than it did at the June. Another guy with tattoos of different types of coffee cups up and down his right arm walked over to join the conversation, and their voices blurred into their version of insider trading, gossip about the restaurants and bars where most of us worked, who was sleeping with who, who was stealing money, who was terrible at their job.

After-hours family, that's what Gabrielle had said, and I was included. A part of it. I loved the word *family*. It occurred to me that I was definitely drunk.

After another beer, another shot, then another, Gabrielle said, "We're going." I thought she was talking about her and Jake, the bartender, but then she stood up, picked up my bag, and handed it to me.

"Aren't we?" she asked, her eyes on mine.

"See you tomorrow," I said to Mike. "Nice to meet you," I said to the Laurel Place–fire girl and the coffee-cup-tattoo guy, neither of whom had introduced themselves to me.

"That bartender," I said as we walked out of the now-crowded bar. The air was cool and crisp. Fall wasn't all that far away, I realized. I hadn't been paying attention.

"What about him?" Gabrielle asked.

"He's cute."

"Do you think so? I would be happy to give him your number."

"You don't have it," I said.

Gabrielle rooted through my bag as we walked, slowing my pace, and pulled out my phone.

"What's your passcode?" she asked. "And who is Noah? You have a text from him."

"Ten-ten," I said. "No one."

"Is he one of Jen's friends?"

"Jen's barely a friend," I said. My voice sounded sharp and hard.

She punched her number into my phone, then put it gently back in my hands. I dropped it in my bag without looking, not sure what she meant by the gesture.

"Most of them are terrible. Boys, I mean," Gabrielle said.

I raised my eyebrows but didn't say anything. We walked around the park, toward my street. "Isn't this where you live? Across from the park?" I asked. I was hungry for more information. I'd already given her my phone passcode. I wanted to be able to imagine where she lived.

"I want to walk you home," Gabrielle said.

I smiled. We walked in a silence that was surprisingly comfortable.

"This is me," I said, fishing my keys out of my bag as we approached my front door.

Gabrielle looked up at the building like she was searching for something or trying to see the moon, invisible behind the nighttime clouds. I thought about my sister somewhere above us, floating on my windowsill. I would have answered any question Gabrielle had asked in that moment. The feeling of her hand in my bag as we walked, reaching for my phone.

"Good night" was all she said. She lifted her arm, and in the dark night air she brought her hand toward me. I thought she was going to reach for my face. I put my hand to my mouth, where the crumb had been just that afternoon. But she just squeezed my shoulder before turning away. I watched as she walked down the street, back to her place on the park. At the end of the block, she turned around, turned back toward me. She lifted a hand and waved.

I unlocked the apartment door quietly. Leo was sitting on the futon in the living room, watching an old movie. An actress and actor kissed in black-and-white. He was twisting something in his hands.

"What are you up to?" I asked.

"Making a bracelet," he said, holding up a tangle of string.

I had such an overwhelming urge to collapse on the futon next to him and ask if he would please, please make one for me that I didn't speak, just nodded, walked into my room, and shut the door behind me. I couldn't stand myself sometimes. My sister was asleep in her jar. I felt inexplicably lonely, almost angry at the sting of it, but I was the one shutting the door. I wished Gabrielle and I were still walking home in the cool dark air.

Later, I walked to the kitchen to get some water. Leo was asleep on the futon, curled on his side. He wore a black hoodie that was enormous on him, like a child in his father's T-shirt. He looked so young in the glow of the movie, still silently playing on the TV screen wedged in the corner, an old love story in black-and-white. The finished bracelet sat on the arm of the futon, woven strands of blue and white that made a patterned band. It was beautiful. I couldn't remember the last time I'd seen something handmade. Leo breathed softly, his eyelashes fluttering in his sleep. I picked the bracelet up, laid it across my wrist, and thought about slipping back into my room. Leo's face was so pale, it almost looked blue. I put the bracelet back on the arm of the futon.

"Good night," I whispered.

The servers, as it turned out, moved as a pack. They went to Juan's kid's eighth birthday party on a Saturday before the evening shift and all showed up at the June just barely on time, a little bit sunburned, buzzy from beers and each other's company. When Mai turned twenty-two, a morning server had covered her shift and everyone else, eager to get cut, hounded Brandon about who he'd release first, then changed into party clothes and dashed off into the night.

Despite the night at Grace's, I was not part of it all, not really. For one, hosts at the June arrived last and left first. The restaurant just wasn't busy enough for us to stay longer. And I had begun to understand that my job required about an hour and a half of actual work. What I was really paid for was to stand politely and prettily at the host stand. Management likes a pretty face, Brandon had said during family meal once.

And also, maybe more important: I was still so new. Everyone else had worked at the June for at least a couple of years. Nobody except Gabrielle, it seemed, had much spare time to spend on figuring out if they could trust me or not. The feeling I got was that my job wasn't strictly necessary. There wouldn't be food without the cooks, and it wouldn't be a restaurant without servers, but if something happened to the hosts, they'd manage. It would be annoying for servers to have to seat the guests, but they'd survive. Plus, I had my sister. I was always asking to be cut early, speed-walking home to check on her. When she'd first returned, she'd almost glowed in her jar on my windowsill. Her scales were fading now, I was sure of it. It gnawed at me, and I knew I came off as preoccupied.

So it felt like a small miracle that Gabrielle pulled me into her orbit whenever she could. And that was how I found myself at a party on the roof of a very fancy apartment building in Chelsea late on a Sunday night.

I hadn't been scheduled for a shift that evening and Gabrielle hadn't texted me the invitation until she was cut. My sister was already asleep in her jar. I felt a bit rebellious, like I was sneaking out after curfew, as I pulled on a pair of loose black jeans that I hoped looked oversize in a stylish way.

When I got there, Gabrielle was drinking red wine out of a red cup. I took a sip. It was cold. Cold red wine—I hadn't even known that was a choice. There was a guy without a shirt

DJing, actually DJing, with vinyl records and beat-up speakers. He played David Bowie, the Supremes, songs I recognized from my grandmother's radio. Gabrielle got me a drink, introduced me to a couple of people she knew—a painter and a graphic designer, people with jobs that sounded made up—then said, "Let's dance." Didn't ask, just said, and then we were dancing with the twelve or thirteen other partygoers on the tiny dance floor in front of the DJ on a roof in Chelsea. A plastic tube appeared in Gabrielle's palm that looked like a bad prop from a Halloween costume for a mad scientist. She tapped a few shards of glass into my hand, except they weren't shards of glass, they were translucent pieces of paper. Gabrielle put two on her tongue, so I did the same. I could see the music, violet and lime green, spinning off the DJ's turntable. We danced, shining with sweat. It felt like everyone was holding their breath, watching us.

When the DJ stopped playing, I turned to Gabrielle. "I need food," I said. She nodded, motioned toward the door, and I followed her out of the beautiful, expensive-looking apartment. We waved to some of Gabrielle's friends as we passed them on the stairs. They smelled like cigarette smoke and sweet night air.

"I can't decide if I'm hungry or not," Gabrielle said as we stood in line at a late-night dumpling place near our neighborhood.

"You're hungry," I said. She laughed and I ordered for us, extravagant for once: twenty-four dumplings and a cold noodle salad to share. We sat in a high-top in the window and devoured the food, our lips glistening from the extra sauce they'd lavished on us. My legs were gloriously tired. We finished, twelve dumplings each, and Gabrielle went back to the counter and returned with two beers and four sweet dumplings with bananas and goji berries baked inside.

"Let's do this every night," I said. "Dumplings at midnight."

"Okay," Gabrielle said through a mouthful of sweetness. I took a sip of beer. The acid we'd taken was making me grind my back teeth together.

"You're so good with people," Gabrielle said. She wiped her mouth with the back of her hand, a little roughly. "Like, you actually seem excited by them. Total strangers. You ask them questions and you listen. Nobody does that, really."

I smiled. I felt anxious around people, mostly; I asked questions in order to fill silence. But that reflected back at me, prismed through Gabrielle, was something good. I stacked the cardboard containers the dumplings were served in and threw them away, returned the plastic tray to the counter.

"Nobody from the restaurant wanted to come?" I asked later as we walked out of the dumpling place.

"Not their thing." Gabrielle shrugged. "I think they were going to Grace's tonight."

I wasn't sure whether to feel stung or reassured that Gabrielle had brought only me along to the party. Was she embarrassed for people we worked with to know we were friends? I didn't think so, but it was confusing that she'd broken from the pack and taken me with her. She didn't walk me to my apartment that night. She hugged me goodbye at the Union Market on Avenue A and Houston. It wasn't until I was climbing into bed later that I realized she hadn't been headed in the direction of her apartment. She'd turned around, walked back. I squeezed my eyes shut, tried to fall asleep fast enough to prove to myself that I didn't care.

The next morning, we left the apartment before ten, my sister in her jar in my tote bag. I was antsy. I wanted to be somewhere, see something, do anything to remember that I was here. I wandered across Houston and sat at a small table outside a coffee shop nursing a latte with milk that wasn't actually milk, at least not in the cow sense. I put my sister's jar on the other side of the table. It was almost like we were two normal human sisters, getting coffee together.

People walked by. Sometimes the sheer number of them was overwhelming—this many people and not a single one sparing us a glance. It almost made me laugh, all these people walking right by a miracle, something magic, my once-dead sister and me, and none of them aware. It was a sunny day and I felt a little drunk on being a person in the world. How strange and singular that was turning out to be.

My phone vibrated on the table, making the water in my sister's jar slosh a little.

"Sorry," I said. "Oh. It's Noah." I held out the phone for her to read.

hey stranger, he'd said.

"I'm going to text back," I said.

She swam her fish body as far from me as she could go.

"I know. But why not?" I replied. "Isn't that why people move here? To fall in love?"

I knew I was kidding myself. Obviously, I was not falling in love with Noah. Dating Noah felt like hedging my bets. But if nothing else was happening, why not him?

Hey, sorry have been MIA. Work is crazy! I typed.

I pressed Send before I could change my mind. I placed my phone facedown on the table and it almost immediately buzzed. A current of water rippled through my sister's jar, just briefly.

thought u worked in a restaurant lol . . . want to grab diner tn

"He spelled *dinner* wrong," I said to my sister. I was a girl sitting at a table talking to her sister-ghost-fish who lived in a pickle jar. I felt a little insane, but there was something to my insanity, as if, for just a moment, I was exempt from embarrassment. My sister did a slow little loop in her jar, her equivalent of the roll of exasperated eyes.

Sounds good, where and when? I typed back.

He responded, *7*, then sent me the name of a restaurant I'd never heard of.

See you then, I wrote. I typed a smiley face, then deleted it. It occurred to me that I should make some friends that I didn't want to sleep with, like the perfectly nice roommates I had. But I hadn't lived here for long. I had a job and my sister, and last night the most beautiful girl in the world had invited me to a party. I had a guy who was taking me to dinner. I would get to it, I told myself. After this.

❧

Noah beat me to the restaurant and was sitting inside, at a table by the window. I tried to pay attention to what my body did when I saw him, but all I felt was a flutter of something. I couldn't decide if the flutter was moth wings of dread or a ping of excitement.

"Hello," I said, sitting down on the chair across from him. I'd dressed carefully for the date: a white linen dress that once belonged to my mother and black sandals. Noah looked irritatingly and objectively appealing, tousled dark hair that he tucked behind his ears, a dark green shirt with artful holes on the seams of one shoulder. It did not seem like appropriate office wear for someone who did something money-related. But then again, what did I know about money?

"What's up," he said. I hated when people said that, *What's up*, without a question mark. Was I supposed to say *What's up* back, nod my chin, or actually tell him what was up? *Not much — my dead sister who is now a fish seems to have some qualms about me being here. What's up with you?*

"Not much," I said. "How was your day?"

"Pretty chill," he said. "Have you eaten here before?"

"No," I said. I tried to appreciate the fact that he'd picked a restaurant in my neighborhood. He'd probably had to take a bus or a train to get here.

"It's good as fuck," he said. "Jamaican. My family goes to Jamaica for Christmas and it is one of the most beautiful places in the world. Better than France or any of that European shit."

I nodded as if I could provide a relevant take. I had never left the country but did not think he would find that attractive.

"The people there are so nice, they love tourists. I'm getting the jerk chicken," he continued without stopping and pointed to his Red Stripe. "Want one?"

I nodded again. "Yes, please." It was becoming very apparent, in the light of day, that this was a poor decision. I noticed he'd taken the hoop out of his nose. I missed it.

"What do you want to eat?" he asked.

I glanced at the menu. "The hot pepper shrimp." It was the second-most-expensive appetizer, which was ten dollars cheaper than the least expensive entrée.

"That's it?" he asked.

"I ate lunch late."

He nodded and walked over to the bar to order, even though there was a server winding her way through the half-empty restaurant toward us. She wouldn't be receiving a tip now, even though we were taking up one of her tables. I wilted a bit in my seat as Noah leaned on the counter, a little too close to the bartender.

Noah returned with Red Stripes, which quickly turned into a pitcher of rum punch, which I hadn't tried before. It smelled like sunscreen and tasted like melted banana Laffy Taffy, straight from its yellow wrapper with the joke beneath the seal.

"What did the egg say to the frying pan?" I asked Noah as I slurped the liquid sunscreen through a pink straw.

He thought for a second. "'You're egg-cellent'?"

"Close. 'You crack me up.'"

Noah allowed a smile and volleyed an equally bad joke back at me, and I exhaled. Finally, something we could talk about: manufactured humor. The food took nearly an hour to arrive and by the time it did, I was buzzy and talkative. Noah spoke about work and I tried to make my brain latch onto the words he was saying, but either I was kind of drunk or hedge-fund communications were endlessly boring.

When we finished eating, Noah sidled back up to the bar to pay, and I exhaled, relieved that he'd picked up the check without asking. A pitcher of rum punch did not currently fit in my budget. I couldn't wait to go home, take off my shoes, and tell my sister she'd been right to roll her eyes. I vowed to make an effort to go on dates with better spellers from now on. I would tell her this. It would make her laugh, my resolution to date better spellers, or it would have if sister-ghost-fish could laugh.

"Want to watch a movie or something?" Noah asked.

We stood on the sidewalk in front of the restaurant. The sky was still light and my head was beginning to thump from the Laffy Taffy punch.

"Um, I don't know. I'm kind of tired."

"You live near here, right?"

"Yes. But I have about a dozen roommates." There was no way Noah was coming to my apartment.

"I don't care," Noah said. "Can we walk from here?"

"And a twin bed," I added. "I have a twin bed. No chairs or anything." My stomach twisted at his insistence, or maybe because of the rum and the spicy shrimp.

Noah laughed. "Seriously, I don't care. If you don't want to hang out, it's fine. You can just get me back for the food later. I'll text you my Venmo."

I did not want to do that.

"We can walk," I said.

Thankfully, nobody was home to watch me walk through the apartment with Noah, or at least no one was in the kitchen or the living room. His eyes looked very big, maybe even concerned, at the giant pile of shoes by the door and the pool of water leaking out from under the fridge. I opened my door and looked apologetically at my sister's jar. She shook her fish head.

"Damn, this room is small," Noah said. He laughed and ran a hand through his hair and sat on my bed; the screws in the cheap metal frame groaned under his weight. My room was not built for boys, especially not boys like Noah, the kind who had memberships at expensive gyms and California king–size personalities.

"What's that?" he asked.

"Don't touch it," I snapped. He was reaching for the pickle jar but snatched his hand away when I spoke, like my voice was something that could slice his hand open.

I reluctantly retrieved my laptop from beneath my bed, where I kept it. "What do you want to watch?" I asked. I sat on the bed beside him, leaving an armful of space between us.

He shrugged. "I don't care. We don't have to watch anything. We could just listen to music or something."

Out of the corner of my eye I saw his hand move toward me and flinched at the thought of him draping his heavy arm over my shoulders, but he just picked up a strand of my hair and examined it.

"You're really pretty," he said without making eye contact. I was still looking at my laptop, pretending to scroll. My sister was shrieking soundlessly, bubbles filling her jar, so many it looked like someone had stuck a straw in the water and blown. He slowly closed my laptop lid, lowered it down until I had to stop pretending to be scrolling through movie options, then gently took the computer from my hands and placed it back beneath my bed.

He leaned forward and kissed me. His breath was sticky and rancid—chicken and stale beer. I scooted back toward the window my bed was jammed up against, toward my sister's jar, away from his mouth. We had hooked up, he had literally been inside of me, but for whatever reason, I could no longer muster a frisson of attraction for him. His body felt so suddenly repulsive, and I wanted nothing more than for him to leave. Shame flared in my chest. I thought about Gabrielle, who would never let something like this happen to her, who would know what to do if she was caught in a small space with someone like Noah.

"What's your deal tonight?" he asked. My heart pounded in my chest. His voice had an edge I hadn't noticed before.

I could feel him move closer to me when I didn't respond. The nearness of his body, the smell of his breath, it was too much all of a sudden. I could barely stand to remain in my body. I wished my skin could detach itself from my body and slither away, go somewhere cold and dark deep beneath the earth. Away from this hot room, the corners of which abruptly came into sharp focus and then started closing in on me. It was hard to breathe.

"Okay," I said. "I mean no. I'm not feeling so good, actually."

He laughed, a weird, awkward sound.

"It's fine," he said. "That drink made my stomach hurt too. We can still..."

He reached for my chest before I could think of a response and squeezed, too hard. His hand there made me flinch and I backed away, but this didn't deter him from moving with me, reaching for the hem of my dress. I was watching the scene unfold from above, as if it were a movie I was not involved in. My brain couldn't or wouldn't click on.

"Wait," I managed, but he wasn't listening, his hand moving beneath my dress without acknowledgment. Somehow I wriggled an arm free. I shoved his shoulder with my hand as hard as I could and he jerked away, into the window, knocking my sister's jar over. The lid fell off, water spread horribly across the floor, and I heard someone shriek. I lunged for the jar, scooped my sister up with both hands, and dropped her back in the half-empty glass. My face was wet and I realized I was sobbing.

"What the fuck?" Noah said, his voice too loud.

"Get the fuck out!" I yelled. I was kneeling on the ground, holding the jar to my chest as he stood over me. "Get the fuck out!" I yelled again and didn't stop yelling until Marcus appeared in my doorway, saw Noah standing over me, grabbed him by the back of his shirt, and dragged him out of our apartment. I put my sister back on the windowsill. She looked okay. Her fish body was moving in and out, breathing. I heard something crash down the stairs. My sister swam a circle in her jar and I let out a long hard breath.

"Are you okay?" Marcus asked, reappearing in my doorway. "He's gone. Do you want me to call anybody?"

I wiped tears from my face, said no, I was fine, just a misunderstanding, thank you, thank you, thank-you-thank-you-thank-you, repeated it until he left and I could collapse fully to the floor, numb with disbelief, humiliated that Marcus was the one to save me from my own bad decision.

"You're okay. It's over," my sister said.

I felt nauseously electric, like I'd brushed a finger against a socket. There was a plastic bag under my bed from one of my trips to the bodega down the street. I pulled it toward me with my fingers, sat up, and vomited into it, then stood up, walked into the kitchen, and filled a jar with water. In my room, I refilled my sister's jar. She'd only lost about half the water. I looked at her and she was floating. She looked normal. Her fish mouth wasn't moving. But her voice had been so distinct in my head, I could almost hear it echoing like the clear sound of the bell back home, the one that rang out every Sunday morning from the Episcopal church just across a parking lot from where we'd lived when we were young and our mother was still alive.

She reached out a fin as if she could wipe the sweat from my forehead, but it brushed against the glass of the pickle jar and she pulled it back to her fish body. I picked up her jar from where it sat on the floor. My hands shook and her water peaked and crested. I quickly put her back down, afraid of dropping her. I would not let anything hurt her ever again.

"Say something?" I whispered.

My sister opened her mouth but only bubbles came out. She shook her head and flung her fins toward the lid of the jar, the equivalent of a shrug. I was still sitting on the floor of my room and I stretched out my legs, lay down next to her. The wood floor was cool on my cheek. My body was rigid with hope. I wanted to hear her voice again. But she just floated in her jar, fins still moving, almost imperceptibly. Her scales slotted together, a pattern like an intricate wallpaper. Eventually I sat up and looked at my phone. It was late, past midnight. My hands were no longer trembling.

"What's the difference between a Duane Reade and a Walgreens?" I asked my sister. We were standing in the home-goods aisle. She looked pale in her jar under the fluorescent lights. I was sweating, for some reason, a sick sweat that prickled my scalp and made me feel nauseated. I wasn't sure why I'd decided to go to Duane Reade at the late hour but I needed to be out of my room, that apartment. For the first time, I'd left the *thank you thank you thank you* tote bag in my room, and her jar was cradled in the crook of my arm. I looked around to see if anyone was eavesdropping on a girl speaking to the glass jar in her arms, but the store was empty besides the security man at the front door and the boy with blue fingernails snapping his gum at the register. I looked back at my sister and caught her rolling her eyes. I rolled mine back.

In my sister's opinion, I cared too much about what other people thought. After our mom died, I was the one who made sure we had lunch boxes from Target and peanut butter and jelly sandwiches like the other girls in school. My sister did not give a fuck about lunch boxes, and it annoyed her that it bothered me when the neighbors whispered about our dead mom and eccentric grandmother.

"What about this?" I asked, picking up a candle with a SALE sticker on it. The overhead light in my room was almost as fluorescent as the lights in the drugstore, a sickly green, and it seemed crucial now, after a horrible day, to fix this, fix something.

I scooped up an armful of those pillar glass candles that made me think of church and held them in the crook of the elbow that wasn't cradling my sister in her jar. The color of my sister's scales had continued to leak away. She'd been the orange of a sunrise when she first floated into my room, and now her color was closer to apricot, but it was okay. It would be okay. She was still there, in a jar in my arms. We walked home, my flip-flops making thwacks that echoed in the quiet city streets.

⁓&⁓

I woke up to a Venmo request from @kingnoah91 for ninety dollars. It read *Uber after party/dinner ln.*

I showed my sister the screen. She rolled her fish eyes.

"Fuck him," I said. She nodded.

I stabbed the red Ignore button with my finger and threw my phone to the foot of my bed as if it were something sick. I could still feel Noah's hand on my chest. I wondered what he would tell Jen. Nothing, probably. I hadn't heard much from her since the party in Bushwick, which felt like a lifetime ago.

Later that morning, when I worked up the nerve to look at my phone again, I had an email from Brandon, asking if I could pick up the host shift that evening. I was still lying on the bed and I could feel my sister reading over my shoulder.

I tried to imagine what my sister would say about Noah if she could speak. About his hand under my dress after I moved away from him.

"He didn't hurt me or anything," I said. "And I'm not telling Jen. That's so embarrassing and I don't think she'd even care."

She gestured with an orange fin, almost translucent, at my phone.

"No. I'm not going. I don't want to leave you."

My sister shook her head. I sighed but she was right. I needed to leave the apartment and not think about Noah, the feeling of being trapped in my room like a caged animal.

"Okay," I said. "What should I wear?"

What I didn't spend much time considering was that my sister had gone through something too. I never asked her if it hurt to fall from the jar onto the hard wooden floor, if it scared her to see what a person like Noah could do. Perhaps I felt guilty that I'd gotten a life and this was what I was doing with it. Perhaps I was just twenty-three and selfish and not at all the person I thought I should be.

I wondered if anyone noticed that I drank almost an entire bottle of the prosecco at after-hours family that night. Nobody was in the mood to go out, so Gabrielle and I walked toward the East Village together and she talked about a book that she hated but couldn't stop reading. She always finished books, a trait I admired but didn't possess. The air had an edge of chill, like winter was ready to swoop in and take over the place. I didn't have much to offer, was content listening to Gabrielle chat on and on, relieved not to be walking home alone. She asked if I was okay when we got to my door and I lied, said yes.

I wondered how different I'd feel if I had texted her instead of Noah the day before.

"Are you sure?" she asked. Embarrassingly, I felt my eyes go hot and wet.

"Oh my god, Alison," Gabrielle said. She reached out as if to touch my cheek, then hesitated. Her hand moved back to her side in slow motion. "What is going on?" she asked.

I felt like a child, near tears and desperate for someone to touch me, just to feel something warm. I couldn't tell her about my sister and didn't want to talk about Noah.

"I'm just feeling a little off," I said. "I've been here for two months now and it still feels, like, temporary or something." I was embarrassed about even saying those words, dull and done before, a cliché.

But Gabrielle nodded. "I don't know if that ever goes away." She studied me, continued, "But isn't it kind of gorgeous that we're here, in the center of it all?"

I nodded. It was kind of gorgeous, to be in her center.

"I'm fine," I said. "I promise. Sorry, I think I just haven't slept much and I drank a lot tonight."

"A bottle of prosecco would make anyone cry. Puke or cry."

I laughed; we said good night. I wasn't sure if New York was my center of the world but if it was the center of Gabrielle's, and I was standing in it, wasn't that something?

❧

"How are you feeling?" I asked my sister the next morning. We were sitting at a table in the park like we did most mornings. I was being less and less careful about pretending like I was on the phone when I spoke to her in public. I didn't care if people saw me on a bench talking to a pickle jar, because it wasn't a pickle jar, it was my sister. And something was wrong. She was continuing to lose color, lose light.

What I really wanted to ask was why she was here, but I was afraid that broke some kind of phantasmic law. If I knew why she was haunting me, would she need to exist?

She sucked in her breath sharply at something behind me and bubbles floated to the top of her jar.

"What?" I glanced over my shoulder. Jen was walking toward us. We weren't far from her apartment but I hadn't heard from her since the horrible, awful night with Noah. Since weeks before then, actually. I pulled my phone out of my bag and pretended to type furiously. I felt her eyes flit toward me as she walked by, but she kept going.

My heart hammered as Jen disappeared into the crowd on the sidewalk. I had the thought that I was totally alone, that I was shaped differently from the people around me. Across the table, my sister swam in a spiral in her jar.

The headiness of summer was gone; fall had crept in quickly. It was my first time living somewhere with such delineated seasons and I was surprised by how fast the trees flamed into color, then began to shed their dead leaves.

My sister still lived in her pickle jar and we spent most mornings going for walks or sitting in the park, she in the jar in my tote bag or cradled in the crook of my arm. She went shopping with me and watched from a corner stool in the dressing room as I tried on black dresses for work. We finished all of *Golden Girls* and started watching *The Sopranos,* which we liked but not as much. We lit candles at night and almost never turned the overhead light on. I tried to forget about Noah and Jen and their horrible little corner of the city, avoiding Jen's street and the purple-painted club. We constructed our own life. I liked living in it.

But at the same time, Gabrielle and I were becoming friends, or something like it. We'd fallen into a pattern that autumn: after-hours family following most of our dinner shifts, then Grace's. We would drink tequila and beer and snort Adderall from her apartment key in the bathroom when Jake the bartender was in a generous mood. We went dancing after Grace's a couple of times, swaying in dark and sweaty clubs with one-word names like East and Nowhere. I missed my sister most while we were dancing.

Gabrielle said that she painted every single day and it was the only time she felt like a real person. She told me that a couple of years ago, she'd fallen in love with a bartender named Charlotte who lived in Bed-Stuy and basically moved into their apartment, but she was so afraid of how much it all was that she hooked up with Jake and the whole thing fell apart. I wanted to absorb every pore of her. I saw something beautiful and I saw something broken and I saw something that seemed like it also saw me.

"What?" I asked one night. We were standing in the sticky bathroom at Grace's, trying to see our reflections in the mirror around the graffiti markered onto the glass. We'd just peed without touching the lidless toilet. She was staring hard at me as if she were trying to find something she dropped into a still, dark pond.

She smiled then. "Nothing," she said. She seemed almost embarrassed I'd caught her searching, except Gabrielle never got embarrassed. In the mirror, I smiled back at her, back at the reflection of us.

❧

One night I got too drunk. I threw up in the toilet at Grace's and then I cried because I was embarrassed that I had thrown up in front of Gabrielle. Tears and snot and vomit came out of my nose and my mouth, and Gabrielle smoothed my forehead with her soft, cool hand.

"You have a hand like a mother," I said.

After that, she took me home to her apartment, her castle near the park. I fell asleep hard on the floor of her bedroom and when I woke up the next morning, my tongue felt coated in sand and none of my surroundings looked familiar.

Her apartment was a two-bedroom on the top floor of the building, that I knew. I tried to recall how I knew this, as I had never been invited in before now, then remembered someone at work had mentioned it one slow night when we were making roll-ups at the bar, folding napkins around forks and knives. Mike and Samuel were going on and on about the places they'd lived since moving to the city, sounding like they were comparing scars. The studio on Sixty-Eighth with a bathtub in the kitchen; the apartment in Bushwick with the toilet in the hall. Mike said then that Gabrielle lived in a two-bedroom apartment on the top floor of her doorman building. He said it with a look that fell somewhere between resentment and condescension, which I found interesting. It did seem odd that Gabrielle, who worked the same job as the rest of us, could afford something so palatial, but she did have an air of good luck or maybe generational wealth about her, something I tried not to think about too much.

I could see the tops of tree branches when I stood up from where I'd slept. Gabrielle had piled pillows and blankets around me so when I woke up, it was like emerging from a soft nest. She didn't have roommates and the apartment smelled like coffee and something clean, lemons. I was wearing a huge T-shirt that said CHILMARK GENERAL STORE. I did not remember changing into the T-shirt. It hung to my knees and I worried the soft hem between my fingertips as I walked from Gabrielle's bedroom to the kitchen. Gabrielle must have helped me out of my vomit-splattered clothes. It occurred to me that it was the first morning my sister-ghost-fish would wake up alone. I felt disgusting.

"Good morning," she said. "You look terrifying."

"I feel terrifying," I replied. "I'm so sorry about last night. That was gross."

Gabrielle smiled. "It's okay," she said.

I liked Gabrielle because she was the kind of person who would say it was okay only if it was. "I hope I didn't say anything embarrassing."

"You didn't say much after you threw up all over the bathroom at Grace's."

I sat on one of the bar stools in front of her kitchen island and said something like "Agh."

"It's fine. Jake deserves to have to clean up some vomit."

Gabrielle was putting ground coffee in a French press that was the size of a small watering can. She was wearing a dark blue camisole with lace on the neckline that looked like something a beautiful woman would wear in a French film and a pair of blue-and-white-striped boxers.

"You talk in your sleep," she said.

"I do not."

"You do. You kept saying something about a sister and pickles. Or a pickle jar?"

I looked hard at her face. Had I said something last night, something strange? "Weird. I don't really like pickles."

"Do you have a sister?" Gabrielle asked. "Or a brother? It's funny, working in a restaurant with someone." She poured water from a sky-blue kettle over the coffee grounds. Steam rose around her face as she continued. "You know how they react to criticism, you can tell when they're drunk, but you can go a year without knowing their last name."

"It is funny," I said. "Not funny ha-ha but funny sad."

"I don't know if it's sad. Maybe there's something that we get from that kind of anonymity, that absence of context, that's good."

My brain felt like it was in knots, a string in a cat's cradle. I was not in the mood to have the dead sister conversation, especially since she wasn't dead, not really. It was November and I had been living in New York for almost five months, my sister was still with me, and it was funny and sad and strange, all of it, that I could move away, form a new life, and still find myself haunted. I was nervous and edgy and suddenly overwhelmed with the need to check on her, on the jar on my windowsill.

"I just remembered to — I have to go," I said. "I'm so sorry for crashing here last night. Thank you again. I love your apartment."

Gabrielle frowned. "You're welcome to stay whenever you like. No coffee?"

"I'm so sorry," I called from her bedroom as I stuffed myself back into my dirty clothes from the night before. "I just totally forgot that I have something I have to go to."

I folded her T-shirt and left it on her white damask coverlet. She made up her bed so tidily, like it was a hotel. I hugged her quickly, then ran down the stairs. It wasn't until I was outside, leaves crunching underfoot, that I realized I hadn't answered her question. Did I have a sister?

My throat was hot and tight and I walked home as fast as I could. I hadn't spent a full night away from her since she'd appeared and I wondered if I'd broken some unwritten rule of her existence. What if she was gone? Or what if something had happened to her? I didn't fully understand it all, so I didn't know how to protect her. My limbs grew heavy as I drew closer. I couldn't make my body move as fast as I wanted it to. I walked past a building with a boarded-up storefront. A poem was scrawled in red paint on the plywood, quite recently done. I could still smell the fumes from the spray can.

> Though a block away you feel distant the mere presence
> changes everything like a chemical dropped on a paper
> and all thoughts disappear in a strange quiet excitement
> I am sure of nothing but this, intensified by breathing

It sounded familiar but I couldn't remember who wrote it. I couldn't remember the title. I could only hear, in my ears, *I am sure of nothing but this, intensified by breathing*. The paint fumes in my head and the words *intensified by breathing, intensified by breathing*. I felt intensified as I walked, hoping, with my fingernails digging into the fleshy parts of my closed fists, that my sister was home.

Finally I was upstairs and through the door. My sister was in her jar.

I picked her up and hugged her to my chest.

"Thank god you're here."

I took a hot shower. I was supposed to work that night, but I didn't want to go. I was exhausted, leveled. I didn't want to let my sister out of my sight. I lay on my bed and pretended to take a nap. I bargained with myself. Five minutes and I would get up. Five more. Two more and I could still make it. Ten minutes and I would text Gabrielle, make up a story about why I was running late.

"Should I skip work?" I asked my sister.

She nodded. She didn't look so good.

"What's wrong?" I asked, but of course, she couldn't answer.

All those years ago, on the day the sea swept her away, I'd wished so hard that it had taken me instead of her. It wasn't fair that my sister was the one who died. But now that we were both here, I wanted to go over to Gabrielle's apartment for a cup of coffee. I wanted to fall in love and dance in a stranger's apartment and write words that meant something to me and go on an airplane. I didn't want to follow the water or trade places with my sister.

"I'll stay," I said. And I did. I watched the minutes tick by on my phone until my shift started and there was no way I could make it. I didn't call. Instead, we watched a movie on my laptop, laughed at the bad acting. My insides felt numb, like nothing. Inside my small room was a whole world; the lamp by my bed glowed honey. I was stuck. I wasn't. I didn't want to go.

I had to. I wouldn't. My room, my sister-ghost-fish world, clung to me, so I stayed, I let it.

⌖

"It is not great, it isn't a good idea, not to show up for your shift," Gabrielle said on the other end of the phone. It was almost midnight and I could hear cars honking, an electric bike speeding past her. It sounded like she was walking home from work or standing outside the June smoking a cigarette. I looked at my sister, asleep in her jar, and turned down the volume on the Tim Burton movie she'd wanted to watch. I knew I would pick my cuticles ragged when I got a paycheck with a missing shift, but I was glad I had stayed in my room with my sister.

"I know, I know. Shit. Sorry. Was Brandon mad?"

"No, I told him you were sick and you texted me to call out because you thought it was my shift as captain."

"Thank you so much, Gabrielle. Seriously." I could sense a tinge of irritation in her voice. "Was it busy?"

"A bit." She sighed. "Are you okay? This isn't like you. You don't really . . . you don't seem like the type to ghost."

I wanted to laugh. It bubbled up in my chest like the hysterical carbonation of a Diet Coke. I tried to choke it down and it came out as a cough. I was not the type to ghost, but I was the type to have one. The ironies were piling up on me.

"Alison? Are you there?"

"I'm here," I replied. "Sorry. I coughed. Yeah, I'm fine. I

really was just sick. I'm fine, though. I'll be there tomorrow night."

"Okay," she said, drawing the syllables out longer than they needed to be.

"Okay. See you tomorrow," I said.

"See you, Alison."

❧

Gabrielle was in the hutch, drinking, when I got to work the next day. I arrived on time, just barely. I had woken up that morning actually feeling sick, nauseated and a little dizzy. I lay in bed until the last minute, until I absolutely had to get up and put clothes on.

"I would offer you some, but..." Gabrielle said.

"Oh, no," I replied quickly. "I'm fine."

"You do look sick," Gabrielle said. Her eyebrows scrunched together and a divot of concern appeared between them. I liked that, her concern. I remembered her mother hands. It was comforting to be worried over, even just a little bit, by a living, breathing, solid person. I felt a wave of nausea and stepped back.

"You need a pick-me-up," she said.

"What?"

"Sit here." She pointed to the upside-down milk crate in the corner. I sat, put my bag on the floor and my sweaty forehead on my knees. I heard her feet, clad in black clogs, leave the hutch. I took deep breaths. Gabrielle walked back a few minutes later and knelt next to me.

"Here," she said. She handed me a teacup on a saucer. A hunk of lemon floated on the top. The tea was so hot, it was steaming, and I caught a whiff of hot sauce.

"I don't think so," I said.

"Trust me. Drink."

I drank. The tea tasted like Tabasco and lemon. It was disgusting for the first three sips, and then I felt so much better that I drank the rest of it noisily. Gabrielle handed me a glass of ice water and I drank from that cup without question, the water so cold it made my teeth ache.

"Better?" she asked. I nodded and my eyes burned. "Thank you," I said through the lump like a pebble from a cold river lodged in my throat.

"Okay," Gabrielle said. "We've got reservations." She squeezed my shoulder and left me in the hutch. I stood up, hung my bag in its usual spot, and went to the host stand. The leather-bound book, our record of reservations, was lying closed on top of the menus for the night. It looked like something sacred and I opened it with the tips of my fingers. We had only three and I was reading the names and times when I noticed a doodle at the bottom corner of the page. It was a simple, tiny drawing in pencil of a fish.

It was a quiet night but I couldn't stand still. I helped bus the outside tables and took drink orders when Juan went on his break. I refilled water glasses, fidgeted with the silverware, warm from the heaters installed above the tables.

I was standing at the host stand wiping pesto stains from the menus when I saw my roommates walking up the block toward me. For a moment, my spirits lifted—they'd known I was having a bad night and had walked over to say hi. Of course, this was impossible, since I barely spoke to them. I had gotten so good at protecting my sister and me, keeping our little corner quiet and safe. Too good at it, maybe.

"Oh my god!" Greta said, skipping up to me when I lifted a hand to wave hello. "You guys! It's our mysterious roommate!"

"What are you up to?" I asked.

"Friend from work has a show at the comedy club on Eighth," Marcus said. Leo nodded, quiet as usual. The four of us talked for a few minutes and I felt myself ridiculously hoping that Gabrielle would come outside to grab a menu or something and see me chatting with my roommates like a normal human who had friends outside of work. She didn't. Eventually Marcus started shuffling his feet, clearly ready to move along.

"We'll text you after!" Greta chirped as they waved goodbye. It was nice of her to say, but she didn't have my number.

At the end of my shift, I clocked out, then went and sat at the bar. It was Gabrielle's night as captain and she didn't care about us breaking the no-staff-on-the-floor-after-shift rule. The kitchen was closed but the bar was still open for a couple of hours, and I liked eavesdropping on the hotel guests. Gabrielle was standing behind the bar, hanging out with Mike. She slid a glass of the nice champagne in front of me.

"What's this for?" I asked.

She shrugged. "Good luck?"

～♐

When I got home that night, the water in my sister's jar was cloudy.

"Are you okay?" I asked, picking her up and holding the jar at eye level.

She shook her fish head no. One dulled fin flitted upward, toward the lid of her jar, like she was gesturing.

"Do you need... fresh water?" I asked.

She nodded. I carried her to the bathroom, turned the shower on, and got in. For the first time, I was grateful for the weak pressure. The water was cool. I still had my work clothes on. I caught a glimpse of myself in the mirror—I looked half drowned.

I took the lid off her jar, crouched down, and carefully poured some of the cloudy water into the drain. We sat in the basin of the tub. I pulled my knees up to my chest and looked at her. My hair dripped onto the plastic laminate in loud plunks, like rain, as the shower slowly filled her jar back up with cool water.

My sister's eyes were red like she was crying, but I couldn't tell for sure. Her fish lips puckered at the fresh, cool water that was slowly filling her jar, but her scales still looked faded. I was struck by the reality of her spectral form. Once she'd been a girl who could run and make banana bread and use her photographic memory to remember the names of birds and trees. Now she was confined to a jar, trapped and wordless.

She looked at me, her eyes wide and pleading. I knew what she wanted, had known, the same way I'd known who she was from the start—even in her spectral form, the impossible reality of my sister, the fish, we didn't need words. We never had. The summer she died, I'd known she was suffering. I'd ignored it. Would I do that again now? I looked at her scales, paler than ever against the linoleum of the shower. She had me, but that wasn't enough. Of course it wasn't. How could I have thought that I could be a whole life for her? And yet.

"I don't know if I can," I said. "I'm sorry. I'm so, so sorry."

Maybe that was the worst part, that I didn't want her to leave. I wanted her to stay even if she was miserable. I didn't want to be alone. I wanted it all: this new life and my sister, here. But I also knew that if I loved her like I said I did, I couldn't have it.

Her jar was full. I reached up and turned the water off.

"Do you have to go?" I asked. My voice like a child's.

She bobbed up and down in her jar: Yes and yes and yes.

I opened my mouth and closed it again without saying anything. I felt hysterical. I felt like throwing myself on the floor, screaming until I laughed, laughing until I broke into six hundred pieces.

"I wish you could stay," I said. "But not if it hurts." We sat there together, quiet, until her eyes lost the panicked look they'd had when I first got home. I carried her back to my room. I hadn't considered the fact that she was probably lonely too. It seemed so obvious now. I put my hand on top of her jar like I was smoothing her hair with my hand, like I used to when we were little and she didn't feel well and would come curl up next to me in bed.

"I promise. You can go back soon," I said. The words were sour leaving my mouth; I could feel grief in my ribs when I said *I promise*. I'd promised. I meant it. I couldn't keep her.

It was one of the saddest realizations of my life, the truth that the love of a family would always contain a grain of obligation. Loving because we had to, not because we chose to. But there was also an entire world between *having to* and *choosing to,* and I'd chosen to love my sister more than any other creature in the world. But if she weren't a fish but a girl in her twenties, if she weren't my sister but a stranger I passed on the street, would I choose this love again, with everything that came with it?

I fell asleep with my hand outstretched, palm open, like I was holding my sister's invisible hand, a hand that no longer existed. I had assumed she returned because she needed me, but for what? I wasn't sure. Perhaps I was wrong. Perhaps I had it all turned around. Perhaps my sister wasn't haunting me — I was haunting her.

Gabrielle was sitting at the top of the steps of the museum, a blue cardboard coffee cup in her hand. I hadn't seen her since my last shift, but she'd texted me the night before, asking if I wanted to meet up at the Met. Of course I did.

She wore a white jumpsuit and sneakers and she was a light-house on the top of the stairs. I hooked my thumb around the strap of my *thank you thank you thank you* tote bag and climbed toward her. For the first time in a long while, the bag did not contain my sister, just my wallet and phone and some loose change. A tube of ChapStick. Ordinary, non-apparition-adjacent things.

We said an anticlimactic hello. I was always anticipating her when we weren't together and it was strange, when I finally did see her, just to say hi. We would spend so much time together in the triangle of work, Grace's, and, sometimes, her apartment, then our shifts wouldn't overlap or she'd take a week off and we would go days without speaking, days that we left unacknowl-edged but that were filled, for me, with the feeling that I was missing out on my real life.

We walked into the museum together and Gabrielle waited for me as a woman in a security uniform checked my bag. I'd felt bad, leaving the apartment without my sister, but I was glad I hadn't brought her. The guard asked me to remove my things from my bag and put them in a gray plastic dish that looked like a dog bowl. Would her jar full of water even have been allowed in? I tried to imagine what I would have done if a security guard told me to throw it away or empty it out. I had a sick image of my hand placing her jar in a black trash bag as Gabrielle and the guard watched. I could feel a headache coming on and blinked hard before rejoining Gabrielle, who hadn't brought a bag. She stood with her hands in the pockets of her jumpsuit.

Gabrielle bought our tickets and we walked toward the left wing, an unspoken agreement between us that she was in charge of this afternoon. A giant hall glowed golden in the afternoon sun. I sucked in my breath. Statues of men with spears and women draped in cloth carved out of stone decorated the room. I had never really thought of statues as being art, but of course they were.

"Beautiful, right?" Gabrielle asked. I just nodded. We spent an hour walking around the museum, around the Greek and Roman art, and then wove through the American wing. My thoughts wandered away from me as Gabrielle looked carefully at a few portraits. I wondered for the zillionth time why she had such a nice apartment, such fancy things, but worked at the same place as the rest of us. I felt gross for thinking about it, but it was hard not to feel vastness between us. I didn't know how to acknowledge it, and I didn't know how to ignore it. It was nearly impossible not to think about money in art museums. It had been nice of her to buy my ticket.

We wandered in and out of rooms for what felt like hours. After the medieval wing, Gabrielle led us to the small café tucked to the side of modern art. We sat by a window in the late-afternoon sun. The days felt startlingly shorter when I wasn't at work. We gossiped about Mike's latest, not very good cocktail creations and Brandon's husband, who had gotten very drunk at the bar at the June the week before.

"Do you have a favorite piece here?" Gabrielle asked.

"I liked the Three Graces downstairs, I think," I said. I was not forming intelligent thoughts in the way I'd hoped I would. I didn't quite get the paintings Gabrielle seemed to like. The portraits were so still and she spent so much time looking at them. But I liked watching her in a place where she was surrounded by beautiful objects and things she loved. I took a bite of my blueberry muffin, and then I saw him. His back was toward me and I tried to swallow my muffin and slide down in my chair at the same time.

"Is something wrong?" Gabrielle asked.

The muffin had turned to cement in my mouth. Gabrielle's face looked narrow with concern. She handed me a napkin and I spit out my bite. She pushed her iced tea across the table to me and I took a sip. He turned and he didn't look like Noah at all, not even close.

"Jesus, did you see a ghost or something? You're so pale."

A ghost, Noah—neither of them was in this café. I opened my mouth, then closed it. I would not tell her anything. I couldn't. I couldn't tell her about my sister, obviously, and I didn't want her to know I was an orphan, that tragic, theatrical word. But I was so alone with all my secrets, everything she didn't know and only I did, and then I was surprising myself and telling her about Noah: his bad jokes, the way he chewed with his mouth open, how he grabbed at me like I wasn't a human being with a beating heart in my chest. I couldn't tell her *every-thing* but it felt so good to confide in her about something.

"I am so sorry, Alison. That's horrendous." Her face looked angry and I was surprised by the relief that flashed through me at her indignation on my behalf. She stood up quickly, knocking her chair over with a loud clatter that echoed through the café. She picked it up without embarrassment and put it back down with such force that the sound of chair legs on tile echoed again.

"Let's go outside," she said. "Let's get out of here."

I followed her down the marble steps and across the sweeping entrance. We sat on the concrete edge of a fountain that was turned off. Neither of us said anything. The sun was going down and for once I felt like something had changed inside of me.

Gabrielle turned to me so we were looking each other in the eye. When was the last time I'd made real, actual eye contact with someone? It was so earnest. I felt like I might cry as I sat there in front of the stupidly perfect museum. *Thank you,* I wanted to say, or maybe, *I love you.*

Instead I said, "Is it too early to go to Grace's?"

"Never," Gabrielle said. "It's never too early for Grace's."

꿏

My sister was swimming in fast, anxious circles in her jar the next day as I got ready for work. I asked if her jar was too small, if I should switch it out for a bowl or something with more space. I walked by a pet store every day on the way to work that had a sign taped to its glass door, handwritten on yellow paper: *No dogs inside pls respecct the cat.* I could buy a big tank. Something filled with marbles or sand. Maybe one of those plastic castles.

She stopped her frantic swimming and shook her head no, furiously. I got the sense that she was trying to tell me something.

"What is it?" I asked, but she just started circling her jar again. Her water was cloudy. Her scales weren't orange anymore, but a light pink like the winter sky at dusk.

"I know we haven't talked about it. I know you need to go. I just don't know what that means," I said.

She bobbed up and down, moving the water in her jar until it looked like it was full of waves, like the ocean.

"I'm sorry," I said. "I don't know what you need."

Marcus and Greta were standing in the kitchen, and as I walked by them, opening my mouth to say goodbye, I realized they were both looking at me very carefully and very strangely.

"Who are you talking to in there?" Marcus asked.

"I heard her in the bathroom yesterday too," Greta said. "Quite chatty."

There was nothing more irritating than someone talking about me in the third person while I was in the room.

"Um." I looked between them. "I'm practicing. I was thinking about joining a play."

"You mean auditioning?" Greta asked.

I looked at her blankly.

"For the play?" Marcus asked.

"Right. That," I said. "Okay, late for work! Bye!"

I was out of the apartment before either of them could speak another word.

It was one of those shifts that was cursed before it even began. The hotel's hot-water heater was broken, which meant ours was out too. The kitchen had to boil water to wash dishes, and the hotel guests were not happy. They were all comped free drinks as an apology, so the bar was slammed and we were running out of glasses. The two busboys were recruited to help in the kitchen, so I was now the host and busser for the evening, and it was, of course, a busy night. Very spicy, by Brandon's scale. By seven, all the tables outside were full. The dining room never filled up completely, at least it hadn't since I'd worked there, but it made people who wanted to sit outside irrationally angry to have to sit indoors instead.

I was at the host stand, gathering myself, when I saw a familiar figure bobbing down the sidewalk toward me. It was November and almost too cold for the host to stay outside, Brandon had said at the beginning of my shift, but we'd try to finish the week off. Apparently, during the winter, the fireplace in the lobby was turned on and we closed the outside seating area.

The figure got closer. It was Jen. It was too late for me to run, so I waved weakly, my fingertips barely breaching the top of the host stand.

"Al!" Jen said.

So we were pretending everything was fine, that it wasn't weird that we'd essentially stopped speaking in the past couple of months.

"How are you?" I asked.

"Good! I'm actually here for dinner! Wait, you work here?" she asked. She had a habit of turning easily gleaned observations into questions.

"Sure do," I said. I felt awkward. Why tonight, of all nights? I didn't have time to speculate on the reasons she hadn't reached out since the summer—maybe she knew what had happened with Noah and maybe she didn't, maybe she was a bad texter, maybe she was a bad friend or a wholly terrible person. But I didn't really care. I just wanted to seat her as quickly as possible.

Brandon did not like it when the staff's friends came to visit, unless they were Mike's friends, C-list celebrities on reality shows with names like Romance Isle who had a penchant for ordering bottles of things.

"Chic!" she chirped. "This will be fun! Can you sit with us for a little?"

"I wish I could, but it's kind of a crazy night."

"Maybe a drink later on!" Jen said.

"Maybe," I said. "Table for two?" I asked, like she was any other guest.

"Oh, no, actually, I think there's going to be, like, five of us? Noah's coming! I hope that's fine?"

I stared at her without speaking for a moment, not sure if I was going to throw up, dissipate into molecules of a human being, or start screaming. Had I summoned him at the museum yesterday? I could feel the cement mixture of the blueberry muffin clogging my throat, a phantom.

"Great! That's great," I said, a little shrilly. It was as if I were watching myself from above, watching the light in myself flicker off as I went into robot-host mode, doing my job automatically as if they were ordinary guests on an ordinary night. "We have plenty of room in the restaurant," I continued. "Did you want to sit now or would you rather start with a drink at the bar while you wait for the rest of your party?"

"Oh," Jen said. "I guess I'll sit now."

I led her through the lobby and the bar, sat her at the booth in the far back corner. Gabrielle's section tonight was the indoor tables in the restaurant, so she would know these were my friends. I wanted to throw the stack of menus I was holding at Jen's head.

"This is so cute!" Jen said. "It looks like a Wes Anderson movie!"

"Enjoy your dinner. The squid-ink pasta is delicious." It was my least favorite thing on the menu. I was feeling mean.

I walked into the hutch and checked my phone, ignoring her chirpy reply. No text from Noah warning me. Did he forget I worked here or was it deliberate somehow? Had it been his idea to come, like enemy forces invading? Was it a weird coincidence or was he trying to get in my head? Either seemed likely.

I looked around but couldn't find Gabrielle. I needed her to know that Noah was coming, but we had reservations to take care of, so I returned to the front and saw Earl and Ernie, a couple in their eighties who'd lived in an apartment across the street since the sixties, waiting to be seated for their regular Thursday-night dinner. I chatted with them mechanically, and when I checked in on the host stand, Jen's boyfriend, Mark; Noah; and two girls I didn't recognize were waiting to be seated.

"Hi, guys!" I said. My voice sounded like cotton candy, gritty, sticky-sweet.

"What's up, Ali," Mark said. He held out his knuckles for a fist bump. I looked at it before touching his knuckles with mine.

"Hi," I said to Noah.

He looked at me with an ambivalent expression. His lips were in a straight line. For a moment, I thought he might just ignore me, which would have been easier, a relief, but then he nodded at me, jutted his chin in my direction.

The two girls said "Hi," "Hi." One of them was Jen's roommate Lauren and the other one said she worked with Noah. I wondered if they were dating. "Noah and I work together" seemed like an odd way to introduce oneself in this situation. I had the urge to ask her if she was okay.

"Let me show you where Jen is seated," I said, gesturing inside.

Mark and Lauren and the girl who worked with Noah walked ahead of me a few steps. Noah walked directly behind me.

"Hey, Alison," Noah whispered, too close to the nape of my neck. His breath smelled like brown liquor, maybe whiskey.

"Why are you here?" I snapped.

"Whoa," he said, and reluctantly, I stopped and turned to look at him. He was holding his palms up as if he were a crossing guard warning me to slow down. "Are you pissed at me?" he asked, looking genuinely confused. "Jesus, sorry. I didn't think you'd care, honestly."

I wondered if that could possibly be true. He looked almost ashamed, like a boy who'd knocked over his mother's favorite lamp and was about to be scolded for shattering something precious.

"Okay," I said. I could be cool. I would be cool. The back of my neck was hot. I hoped Gabrielle wasn't around. "This is where I work," I said. "So. Behave."

He rolled his eyes and nodded, but his lips quirked up in a smile that roiled my stomach. I was both relieved and a bit disgusted with myself for brokering a kind of peace with him instead of saying what I actually wanted to say, which was *Who the fuck do you think you are?*

Be careful, I reminded myself. I placed menus in front of them, flashed a weak smile, and fled back outside to the host stand. I would not reenter that restaurant until they left, not even if it started raining fire. I gripped one of our cheap plastic pens so tightly, it started to splinter.

I tried to forget that the man who had been flung out of my apartment by my roommate was eating dinner in the restaurant where I worked. A man who'd pinned one of my arms to a wall and grabbed at me like some kind of creature. I tried to catalog my emotions gently, with the tips of my fingers. For one minute a few months ago, I'd thought he was someone I could try to fall in love with. But now I just wanted to do my job and then I wanted to go home and sleep for a very long time.

"Are those your friends at one-oh-three?" I turned and saw Gabrielle standing at the top of the steps. She didn't look angry, exactly, but something was definitely wrong.

"Um, no. Well, kind of. Jen is, and I know Mark, her boyfriend. And the guy with the dark hair is Noah."

"That's Noah? Are you fucking kidding me? Why is he here?"

"I have no idea. They just showed up."

"Fuck," she said, her voice sharp and a little scary. "They're super-drunk. They've broken two wineglasses already and they haven't even finished their apps yet. I would try to keep Brandon from finding out that they belong to you."

"They don't belong to me!" I said, but she was already turning and walking up the stairs. The inside of my body felt crackly with electricity. I knew Gabrielle wasn't mad at me but sometimes when she was stressed at work, it was hard not to take her personally. I hated that Gabrielle was their server.

It did not rain fire but eventually I had to bus a table outside and take the dirty plates and glasses to the bus bin inside the restaurant. I tried to drop the dishes in the bus stand without their table seeing me. Jen was telling a story that involved a lot of hand motions. Everyone was laughing very hard and loud. There were several empty bottles of wine on the table.

"Al! Come here!" Jen called.

"Hi, guys," I said. I felt summoned, like a maid. "How's everything?"

"So great!" Jen said. "The food is so much better than you said!"

I winced, praying nobody I worked with overheard her. I hadn't talked to Jen, not really, since I started working here. I had never said anything about the food to her.

"So glad to hear it!" I walked around the table closer to Jen and said in a low voice, "My manager is kind of strict here, so if you guys wouldn't mind just, like, being careful." I felt my cheeks redden, humiliated, felt like a schoolteacher scolding her students, but I couldn't afford to lose this job or pay for the broken glasses.

"Oh," Jen said in a loud stage whisper. "Totally. On it."

"Thank you so much," I said. "I hope your dinner is delicious."

Gabrielle and Mai were standing in the hutch talking to Mike through the drink window. They stopped speaking when I walked in.

"Those people are terrible," Mike said. "One of them asked for a dirty Manhattan with an extra cherry."

"What the fuck is a dirty Manhattan," Mai said.

Gabrielle gave me an apologetic look. I was grateful she hadn't told Mai and Mike they were my friends. Or, not friends, but people I knew.

"I'll tell you what a dirty Manhattan with an extra cherry is," Mike said. "It's whiskey, vermouth, olive juice, bitters, and a *cherry*." He looked distraught.

I thought about Gabrielle and me standing at the bar at Grace's, comparing ideas for tattoos we would never get. I thought about Gabrielle smoothing my hair back when I'd gotten sick, then covering for me at work the next day.

They finally left at midnight.

"Ali!" Jen said as they walked down the stairs. "Meet us for drinks at the Cellar when you get off!"

I didn't attempt a smile, just said, "Maybe," in a tone that meant *Absolutely not, we will likely never speak to each other again.*

Noah stopped at the host stand as they were walking away. "Will you come?" he asked.

"I won't be off for a while," I said. "So probably not."

I didn't know why I couldn't just say *No, fuck off,* to him. I just stood there, clenching my fists and trying to smile.

He was standing close to me, too close, and before I realized what was happening, he was kissing me, his front teeth clumsily connecting with mine. I pushed him off and walked a few yards down the sidewalk, away from the guests and the front windows of the hotel. He followed.

"Get away from me," I said. My hands were trembling and I balled them into fists so he wouldn't see. "I'm working. I work here."

His face was red. He was embarrassed and he stood still in front of me, waiting—for what? For me to make him feel better?

"Leave. Or I'll call security," I said. We didn't have security, but it was a threat I'd seen Gabrielle use on handsy barflies who'd overstayed their welcome.

"Fine, Alison. Whatever." He turned and retreated down the sidewalk, following the rest of his pack.

"Are you okay?" Gabrielle appeared like a ghost.

I nodded.

"I'm sorry I snapped earlier," she said. "I shouldn't have done that. I'm so sorry he came here. What an absolute, genuine loser he is." I could tell she was trying to cheer me up.

"It's okay," I said.

"They split the bill five ways," Gabrielle said. "So annoying."

I saw the receipts sticking out of her apron. She hadn't closed them out yet. I reached for them before I could think about what I was doing or why, but Gabrielle turned before I could snag them.

"Let me see," I said.

"No. It doesn't matter. They're gone," she replied.

"Gabrielle," I said. "Let. Me. See." I rarely insisted on

anything and was almost surprised when Gabrielle handed them over. Written in precise letters on the receipt with the name Johnson, Noah S., underneath the signature line: *Alison is a gross whore who owes me ninety dollars, please deduct that from my bill,* a sick little smiley face drawn beside it.

My face got hot. Gabrielle said something to me that I couldn't hear over the humiliation whooshing through me. I handed the receipts back, but not before noticing that not a single one of them had left a tip. Just then, Brandon banged out of the door to the kitchen.

"That table was nightmarish," he said, kind of laughing. "Jesus. Since neither of you seem to be doing much work at the moment, you can clock out if you'd like. The kitchen's closing now."

"Thanks, Brandon," Gabrielle said. I just nodded.

"I'm so sorry," I said to Gabrielle after Brandon went back inside. I was relieved he didn't actually seem to be upset with either of us.

"Wait a sec for me to close out?" she asked. "We can go to Grace's after. You need a drink."

I shook my head no. "I have something to do," I said. "I'll see you later."

I clocked out, picked up my bag, and walked up the stairs and out the employee exit. I stood on the street in the black shift dress I had worn to work with my black clogs. The dread inside of me was melting and turning into something hot. Instead of turning left, toward home, I went right.

The Cellar was half a block from the June. It was on the same side of the street. They had, after all, told me where to find them. They had invited me along. What had they thought would happen? What did *I* think was going to happen? As I walked, I felt like I was growing taller. I swung open the glass door. It was expensive and speakeasy-themed, a place Mike and Gabrielle made fun of regularly. Jen and Mark were sitting at the bar. When Jen saw me, her eyes got big.

"Ali!" she said. "Wow. We didn't think you'd come."

"What the fuck is wrong with you, Jen?" I asked. I had never spoken to her like that. I had really never spoken to anyone like that. My heart felt heavy and red in my chest, like I could do anything, run sixty miles without stopping.

Her mouth hung open for a second before she caught herself, readjusted. "It was just a joke, Alison!" she said, her voice too loud. "He was just kidding around!" she almost shrieked.

"Okay, okay, chill," Mark said. "Noah told us you thought it would be funny. He said you, like, never Venmoed him back or something." I ignored him.

"I thought I was going to get fired. I almost *did* get fired. Do you know how many things you broke? How much money those glasses cost?" I demanded. "Do you think I make a lot, working there? I'm not even a server."

I could hear my voice getting louder, echoing around the dark room. I hadn't taken my eyes off Jen. She was fidgeting in her seat, trying to scoot away from me. She hated a scene.

"What do you want me to say, that I'm sorry?" she said. "Sorry, okay. It was a bad joke. If you need money, we'll give you money. Jesus."

A part of me felt satisfied at this rare sight, Jen letting her saccharine false self slip a little. I liked it when she revealed who she really was. She was mean and she was selfish, but at least it was real. It was a better look on her, honesty.

"Where's Noah," I said flatly, not asking.

"It doesn't matter, Ali," Jen said, shaking her head. "Just go home."

Maybe it was the way she shook her head, but in that dark and tacky bar, I realized that she knew about Noah. Maybe not the specifics, but she knew her boyfriend's best friend had done something horrible to me and to who knew how many other girls, some of them probably also her friends. She knew and there was nothing she would do. We'd grown up in the same bleak place, but she'd found a golden corner of New York, an apartment with a staircase, and friends who kept Adderall in the pockets of the Carhartt pants they wore ironically, and she was not going to risk that, not for me, probably not for anyone. I could almost understand it. Almost, except if Noah treated me like a paper doll, it made me wonder how many other women he'd ripped in half, left behind like uninteresting toys, or worse. It made me wonder how Mark treated her. I was almost sad for her.

I walked to the back of the bar and pushed open the swinging door to the men's room. My vision was sharp; adrenaline thrummed through me. I felt like I was the villain in someone else's bad dream, like I could put a curse on someone.

Noah stood at the sink washing his hands. Our eyes met in the mirror before I said a word. He didn't flinch.

"Oh, good," he said. "You made it."

"Why?" I asked. "Why did you start this in the first place?"

He took a step toward me.

"So you've forgotten that dinner I bought you? Those drinks?" He scoffed. "*You* strung *me* along, Alison. I didn't do anything you didn't want. You're the one who started acting like a psycho. And now you're the one who followed me into the bathroom at a bar." He let out a hard laugh. "Do you want more? Is this some kind of game we're playing?"

I heard a roar in my ears like a storm, the ocean. The *o* in the word *psycho* a tunnel. I was clutching my phone in my right hand and then my arm was cocked back and then I was throwing it at him. I don't think I truly expected to hit him, but to my surprise, and to his, the phone collided with the inside corner of his left eye and his nose and then he was bleeding. As it hit his face and fell to the floor, it started ringing. In fact, the bleeding and the ringing seemed to begin at the same time.

"Fucking bitch!" he yelled, kneeling down and cradling his injured head.

I collected my phone from the tiles, delighted to see that the screen had remained intact, wiped it on the front of my dress, and said, "Hello?" as I walked out of the bathroom. I was shaking, but I felt like I had some magical, mysterious power that I was finally able to access. I was happy to let Noah have the last word. I wasn't the one bleeding from my nose in the dirty bathroom of a bar.

"Where did you go?" Gabrielle's voice asked. "Are you okay?"

I smiled. "I'm fine," I said. "Are you at Grace's? I'm free after all. I'll come meet you."

⁓

The next morning, I was woken by a loud knock at my door.

"Amanda!" a voice said. Marcus's. "Sorry — I mean, Alison? Someone downstairs is trying to buzz in for you!"

I rubbed my eyes. "Coming!" I said. I had fallen asleep in the dress I'd worn to work the night before. It had a little spatter of blood on it from Noah's nose. Or maybe it was ketchup.

I pressed the button for the intercom that was located, oddly, above the sink. I realized it was the first time someone had buzzed up for me.

"Who is it?" I asked.

"It's Gabrielle. Come for a coffee."

I was hungover. We'd stayed out late the night before and I barely remembered getting home. Gabrielle had laughed so hard she almost peed when I told her I threw my phone at Noah's face. I started drinking gin martinis after that, basking in the glow of her laughter. My head hurt.

"Please," she said. My finger was still pressing on the intercom button.

"I'll be down in a minute," I said.

I took my time brushing my teeth, then dressed in black jeans and a gray sweatshirt and my black boots.

"I'm going to get coffee with Gabrielle," I said to my sister. "I'll be back soon. Maybe we can go to the park?" I hadn't told her what happened with Noah, and I felt bad for leaving her in the dark. We hadn't figured out yet how to free her, how she could move on, but Gabrielle was downstairs. I couldn't say no.

"Good morning," Gabrielle said. I crossed my arms. She stood on the sidewalk next to a chair with three legs someone had discarded, smoking a cigarette. "Let's walk."

"I am so hungover," I said.

I followed Gabrielle across East Houston to a café with the name BLACK DOG painted on a wooden sign. We walked down the stairs. It was hot inside, like an oven left on, and quiet. We stood in line without making small talk and I wondered if she was hungover too. It was hard to imagine her feeling as bad as I did. When we got to the front, Gabrielle asked for a cappuccino.

"My treat," she said, turning toward me.

"I'll have tea with milk and sugar," I said. "Lots of milk."

I knew it wasn't cool—milk, sugar, tea—but I was tired of the bitter, tired of trying to prove myself to a city full of black-coffee drinkers. I wanted my tea sweet, I wanted to say things that ended in an exclamation mark, I wanted to see a movie with either a superhero or a love story. I was so tired of contorting myself to fit into places when nobody was even watching. We sat with our drinks on a couch that was low to the ground. It was red and smelled mildly like a wet dog.

"God," I said out loud, looking out the big café window at the street, the people going in and out of stores, cafés, apartments. So many people. "What am I doing here?"

"Everyone who lives here wonders that at least once a week. It's impossible not to," Gabrielle said.

"I feel like you people know something I don't."

"We're only better at pretending."

"I'm good at pretending," I said.

"You're not as good as you think you are," Gabrielle replied and I opened my mouth to respond, but she spoke first.

"I think it's beautiful that you don't pretend, even if it's because you can't because you don't have a poker face," she continued. "You're not a bluffer, your emotions are always on your face, but it makes it easy to like you. People feel easy around you. Haven't you noticed that?" She took a sip from her cappuccino, crossed one leg over the other. "It's why I liked you when I met you. I knew I'd never have to guess."

I bit the insides of my cheek, trying not to grin at that, feeling glowy and awkward all at once. My elbows felt pointy against the couch cushions, like they didn't belong to me. I had not noticed, ever, that people felt at ease around me. I wanted to wrap my arms around her but instead I put down my tea and slid my hands beneath my thighs.

"So, do you have, like, family?" she asked suddenly. I didn't know what to say. The warm glow drained from my face. Could she sense the loneliness on me, acrid, almost tangible? Was it that obvious that I was alone?

"I mean family you'll go home to for Christmas," she said, studying my expression. God, I was sensitive.

"Oh. No, I'll probably stay here." I hadn't thought much about the holidays yet. I assumed I would be working.

"My family has a house in Florida," Gabrielle said. "Nobody will be there at Christmas, so it would just be us." She paused. "What would you think about going?" I blinked.

"To Florida? For Christmas?" I asked. Saying yes meant so much more than *yes*. It meant Gabrielle and I would be friends who traveled and spent holidays together, not just work friends. It also meant leaving my sister alone in her jar for days, maybe even a week. My sister, who was already fading. I couldn't— there was no way.

She laughed. "Yes, to Florida. Key West. Have you been?"

"That's such a nice offer, Gabrielle, but I don't think I can afford that right now." Which wasn't a lie.

She frowned. "Well, we could leave on Christmas Day, so plane tickets will be less expensive. And you won't have to pay for anything once you're there. We'll lie in the sun and get gorgeous and tan and not think about snow for a week."

"I don't know."

"Think about it, at least? Please? I really want to go but I don't want to spend Christmas by myself."

"Okay, but—"

"Okay!" Gabrielle said. "Just say okay." I hadn't seen her like this before. She seemed almost nervous.

"I'll think about it. I promise."

She smiled, stood up, and reached out a hand to pull me up from the couch, and we walked in the direction of home, together.

⟿

When I opened my bedroom door, I could see puddles of water on my floor. My sister sat at the bottom of her jar.

"Where is all of this water from?" I asked. I picked up a dirty T-shirt from the end of my bed and my hands shook as I started mopping it up. Something was wrong with her. I tried to collect everything I knew: Her fading scales, cloudy water. The way she spun through her jar, using her body to make waves.

"Gabrielle invited me to go to her house in the Keys for Christmas," I said.

My sister's fish eyes got big and she started swimming in zippy, happy circles again. I was confused. Why would she want me to leave her?

"But is that weird? We haven't known each other for long. And I wouldn't want to leave you here for the holidays."

Her face fell, somehow. Her water was cloudy and her scales were almost pink, like salmon. The room was filled with a salty, briny smell, like oysters.

I stared at the water on the floor.

"Is what you need water?" I asked. "To go back to the ocean?" It seemed almost too obvious.

She bobbed up and down. *Yes.* A door inside of me slammed shut.

"You want to go to Florida?" I asked. She bobbed up and down, a vigorous yes. Yes and yes and yes.

"That will...help you? To go?" I asked. *Yes. Yes.* My heart was pounding.

"I don't know. I don't know if it's a good idea. Are you sure? Why Florida?"

She put her fins in front of her like she was praying or begging. I had promised. I had promised. It made me feel sick to my stomach that my sister was begging me to help her. Again. Could I do this to her again, deny her what she needed?

No. No, I couldn't.

She blew bubbles in her pickle jar and I could almost feel warm, salty air bend around me, as if she were hugging me, enveloping me in whatever not-unreal thing she was.

I texted Gabrielle.

We're in, thank you so much for the invite. Can't wait for Florida!
She responded almost instantly.

Amazing! Had a feeling you were a yes ... bought plane tickets w miles so dw about that. Christmas gift from me to you :)

Before I could respond she texted again.

Wait ha ha who's we?

I was getting worse at keeping my sister-world and my Gabrielle-world separate.

Me and you! I wrote back. Then sent a :)

See you at work xx, she responded.

"We're going to Florida," I said to my sister. She swam circles in her jar. I smiled, and it felt watery, fake.

I locked my phone and shoved it under my pillow where I kept it every night. It would likely give me brain cancer one day. I closed my eyes, worrying about my sister, worrying about Gabrielle, worrying about my brain. And then I took my phone out and replied *xxx* before getting up and dressed for work.

The hotel and, by extension, the restaurant had gotten busy after Thanksgiving. I picked up an extra shift, then another, and by December I was working almost every day. I didn't mind. Gabrielle was working a lot too. We stopped going to Grace's as much and would walk through the cold dark to her apartment after work instead. There was always leftover pizza or a hunk of cheese in her refrigerator and something for us to drink, fancy tequila or red wine from Trader Joe's. Sometimes when she got drunk, she would put on a record and sing in the kitchen while she washed our wineglasses or plates. Her voice when she spoke was husky, like she was recovering from a cold, but when she sang, it was delicate, the thin lip of an expensive wineglass. It was in those moments, alone in her kitchen or walking home from work, that I realized I didn't know much, almost nothing at all, about her life before New York. Every once in a while, I would ask, "How many languages can you speak?" or "Does your family live nearby?" and she would laugh and change the subject. I didn't mind; I did the same. It was one of the things I liked most about my new life — if I wanted to use an eraser, wipe out anything that came before, I was allowed. I didn't have to answer questions about who I had been.

Sometimes I would fall asleep at Gabrielle's apartment after work. Not often — I hated leaving my sister alone for long and I already felt guilty that I was working so much. But Gabrielle had an open kitchen with an island that looked over her big living room, where a turquoise velvet couch and two overstuffed armchairs sat on a fluffy rug from Morocco in the middle of the room. She slept in one of the bedrooms and used the other as an art studio. I would pass out at her apartment during our after-work aperitifs, legs hooked over the arm of one of those great big chairs, and she would drape her blue afghan over me and let me sleep. I loved waking up in her apartment, the smell of espresso and oil paints wafting through the big room. When I was there, it was as if she'd cast a magic spell and nothing could bother us. It was like we lived on an island, safe from any wicked thing that might stir the ocean surrounding it.

But of course, I didn't live there. I lived a few streets away, in a tiny bedroom with my sister-ghost-fish. And I was behaving badly. The closer we got to Christmas, the less I wanted to be around her. It was so obvious what I was doing, so similar to what I *had* done. She'd sunk behind a blue curtain and something in me could sense the darkness, so I'd squeezed my eyes shut. I didn't want to watch the world lose her again.

I got the sense that my sister was curious about Gabrielle. On the nights I slept at her apartment, I always left early the next day, not wanting to be in the way while she painted. I felt a desire to shield my sister from Gabrielle, and Gabrielle from my sister, so I never said much to my sister when I got back, as opposed to when I came home from work, when I'd give her a full report. I wanted to keep them separate, safe. I couldn't tell Gabrielle that my sister haunted me in the form of a fish, a fish who lived in a pickle jar on my windowsill, the most obvious reason being she would think I was crazy. But also, I would not give anyone an opportunity to hurt my sister, to wish her away, to vanish her with their words. Nothing could erode how protective of my sister I was, my hard, rocky loyalty. I couldn't love someone who didn't believe in her. So it was better for Gabrielle not to know she existed.

At some point before Christmas, I realized I didn't have a bathing suit. I'd spent most of my childhood in the water, and now I was a girl who lived in a city and had no bathing suit. I checked the Goodwill near the June, then a store in the East Village where I'd picked out clothes for work when I first moved to the city. It felt like a million years ago. I wandered the aisles, the distinct smell of thrift store simultaneously giving me a headache and making me feel at home. I bought a pair of sandals, worn brown leather with strings that tied around my ankles, but there were no bathing suits. I took a bus filled with holiday shoppers and their children to an Old Navy near Madison Square Garden. There was one black bathing suit in the entire store and it was on the sale rack, a one-piece that tied at the neck. It was a size too big, but I bought it anyway.

I hadn't left the city since I'd arrived, not even to go to one of those little towns upstate that everyone loved talking about during the fall. It still hadn't snowed and every day was gray: gray sky, gray clouds, even the sidewalks were a grimmer gray than they were in the summer. It was wearing on me, making me feel thin-skinned and irritated. And the cold air was making my hands and face and feet dry and itchy. I almost missed the humidity of home. I was getting snappier with customers at work. I told a couple there was a ninety-minute wait for a table because they were impatient and condescending, and they left the restaurant. Dealing with impatience and condescension hadn't been covered by Mai during training, but I was pretty sure Brandon would not be happy if he found out I was turning customers away. Still, I dreaded leaving for Florida. I wasn't sure if I could face being in New York afterward without my sister. I had come to the city alone; that I would have to return alone again felt impossibly cruel.

I worked the dinner shift on Christmas Eve, the night before we left. Gabrielle was off and I wondered what she was doing as I dropped dirty dishes into the bus bin and pulled shots from the espresso machine. It felt asymmetrical that she was likely folding expensive linen tops into an expensive bag while my sister swam in circles in her jar in my cold bedroom.

It was her last night in the city and we were apart. I hated that. I wished I had thought to switch my shift, but I'd had a hard enough time finding someone to cover for the seven days we were going to Florida.

We were leaving early the next morning and Gabrielle texted me before my shift ended to say she would pick me up at six. I hadn't mentioned to her that I was bringing a fish or what would look to her like an empty jar of water. I was planning to tell her it was my reusable water bottle.

"I hear you're going on vacation," Juan said to me as I stood at the barista station making myself a cup of espresso.

"Florida," I replied.

"I have some family in Florida," Juan said. "I'm happy you're going; you will have a wonderful time. It's good to get a break from this place," he said, gesturing. I wondered if he meant the restaurant or the city. Both, maybe.

"I think so too. I haven't left since I moved here."

Juan nodded. "So Gabi has taken a liking to you, yes?" Juan asked.

I felt a weird thrill at hearing that come out of his mouth. A warm thrill. "I don't know," I said, trying to be coy. "Has she?"

"She has," Juan said, looking straight at me. He opened his mouth, then closed it again.

"What?" I asked.

"You can't tell anyone that you know this. Not even Gabi, especially not her."

"Okay," I said.

"Her father owns the restaurant," Juan said. "The entire hotel, actually, and more."

"Oh," I replied. I was both surprised and not. She had an air of money about her. I hadn't been able to figure out why a girl with emerald rings and an apartment near the park waited tables. Of course her dad owned the hotel. I was surprised I hadn't thought of that.

"That's not such a big deal, right?" I asked.

"She thinks no one knows, she doesn't want to be treated differently, but her family is rich. Very rich. Or so I've heard." He flicked his palms up in a *Who knows?* gesture.

"I don't mean to gossip," he said. "And I would never want to upset Gabi. She is very dear to me."

"I get it," I replied. I wasn't sure what he wanted me to say.

"I just thought it might be nice for you to know. Before you go, so you aren't surprised."

"Okay. Thank you," I said.

"We love her," Juan said, like a warning. I thought he'd say something like *So don't hurt her* next, but instead he said, "She is a special one."

I nodded. I felt like Juan was expecting a bigger reaction from me, but mostly I wondered when, if ever, I would be included in the royal *we* of the June.

He walked away to check on one of his tables before I could reply.

My walk through the city that night, back toward my sister, my apartment, felt like a knot that kept growing tighter and tighter. I stopped at a deli to get snacks for the plane. I walked an extra lap around the park to look at the lights someone had strung haphazardly on the trees. I did a terrible job of trying not to think about how this would be the last time I walked from work to my home and my windowsill where my sister lived.

When I got back, Greta and Leo were sitting on the futon, watching a movie.

"You're still here!" Greta said.

"We thought you left for Christmas," Leo said, his voice barely above a whisper.

"Or whatever holiday you celebrate," Greta added. Leo nodded.

"I'm not leaving until tomorrow," I said. I didn't clarify that I wasn't going to my home. I didn't say how much I wished I were staying in that cramped apartment instead of going to Florida.

"Did you get the part?" Leo asked.

"What?"

"In the play!" Greta said. "What was it, *Hamlet?*"

"Oh. No. I didn't."

"You'll get the next one," Leo said. "I'm sure of it."

PART TWO

THE NEXT MORNING, my room was so cold that my bones felt like metal. At 5:50, I picked up my packed bag, nestled my sister in her *thank you thank you thank you* tote, and walked downstairs to wait for Gabrielle in the foyer of my building.

It was Christmas. Usually I dreaded this day so much that I would spend the month prior numbing myself. I avoided anyone who might ask what my plans were for the holidays, skipped stores that twinkled with holiday music and trees, ate Chinese takeout and watched TV shows about murder. This year I felt neutral, or at least not afraid of how the day would illuminate my aloneness. It was impossible not to think of my beautiful mom on Christmas, my sister, my grandmother, but this year, I imagined my mom wherever she was knowing my sister and I were together, going on a trip. She would be so happy just to know that.

"Are you excited?" I asked my sister through the thick fabric. "I can't believe we're going on a plane."

A black car with an Uber sticker on the windshield pulled up to the curb. Gabrielle cracked the window and waved, then rolled it back up. I ran from the lobby through the cold air and jumped into the back seat, put my duffel bag on the floor and my tote bag in my lap.

"Hi!" I said. "Merry Christmas."

"Hi," Gabrielle said.

I felt shy, for some reason, and I could tell she did too. She leaned toward me and for a wild moment, I thought she was going to tell me to get out, that the trip was off. I could feel the heat of her body close to mine.

"What is that?" Gabrielle asked, looking at my tote bag.

She reached her hand out and pressed a finger against the hard lump in my bag, where my sister was currently floating in her Mt. Olive kosher pickle jar that hadn't held pickles for months. I couldn't imagine it ever being a vessel for pickled cucumbers, it so absolutely belonged now to my sister. The jar contained my sister-ghost-fish and 3.4 ounces of water, exactly the amount TSA would allow on a plane.

"You're sloshing," she said.

She was right.

"Oh," I said. "It's my water bottle."

My sister and I had spent hours over the past week trying to decide how we would get her to Florida without causing a scene. Since she was in a glass jar full of water but nobody could see her but me, we landed on the pickle-jar-as-upcycled-water-bottle idea. I was eco-conscious! It seemed plausible. It was certainly easier than telling Gabrielle I was excited about the vacation but also using the proximity to the Gulf of Mexico to help my sister return to the great beyond or heaven or wherever it was she was going.

"Will they let you bring that on the plane?" she asked. "I think you can only take, like, three ounces of water through security."

"Three point four," I said.

"What?"

"It's three point four ounces of liquid you're allowed to bring on a plane."

"Oh. Okay." Gabrielle gave me a weird look but didn't say anything else.

The driver pulled away from the curb and pointed the car toward the airport. We were quiet. It was so early and so still in the city, and the hush was somehow contagious. We drove over the Williamsburg Bridge and the city sprawled out all around us in its glittery chaos while the East River moved beneath it, looking absolutely bottomless. New York didn't feel like mine, maybe it never would, but in the hush of a quiet city, it was beautiful. I looked over at Gabrielle to see if she saw it too, how endless and sharp it all was, but she was asleep with her head against the window. Her eyelids twitched as if she were dreaming. I hoped she wasn't annoyed with me already. I peeked into the bag to check on my sister in the jar on my lap. She was asleep too.

When we arrived at JFK, the airport was busy. Businessmen in serious blue suits, bristling with irritation at the inconvenience of the real world; families with tired faces, young children, and tote bags filled with wrapped presents; a small group of schoolchildren all dressed in blue T-shirts, lanyards around their necks. It smelled like carpet and stale coffee.

"I didn't think it would be this busy. Are you checking a bag?" Gabrielle asked.

"No, I just have this," I said, gesturing at the black duffel I'd used as a suitcase since high school.

"I'm going to check mine, but I have precheck for security, so do you want to go ahead and I'll meet you on the other side?" she asked.

"Sure," I said.

She yawned. "Christ, I need a coffee. I'll see you in a bit."

I got in line for security, holding my hand protectively on my tote bag. As we got close to the front, I removed my shoes and the winter coat I wouldn't need for the next week. I was surprised at how loud it was: families with small, chattering children, TSA agents loudly broadcasting reminders about removing laptops from bags. My forehead prickled with a cold sweat. I put my duffel and tote bag and shoes in a parade of plastic bins.

"See you soon," I whispered, trying to move my mouth as little as possible, hoping my sister could hear me. I got in line for the intimidating gray full-body scanner and tapped my sock-clad toes, ready for this part of the trip to be over. I made a mental note to wear matching socks next time I went on a trip by airplane.

I was standing in the crowd of travelers waiting for our bags to be spit through the x-ray machine when a tall woman in a blue TSA uniform yelled, "Who does this belong to?"

She was holding my sister in her pickle jar in a blue-gloved hand and shaking the jar in the air. My tote bag was open on the metal table in front of her. My sister looked terrified.

"Me!" I yelled, raising my hand. "It's mine!"

I raced over, distraught at the sight of my sister being rocked in her jar. The agent rolled her eyes as I hurried toward her.

"You can't have more than three point four ounces of liquid. This look like three point four ounces of liquid to you?" She shook the jar at me.

"Um. Yes, actually. I thought so?" I couldn't look anywhere but at my sister, rocking back and forth in the water.

"You thought so?" She glared at me. "I can either dump it out and give you the jar back or you can throw the whole thing away."

"No!" I yelped as if I'd been pinched. "Sorry. I mean—" I tried to think. "I measured, like, three times. I really thought that was three point four ounces."

"It's not. Dump the water or throw the jar out?"

"Can you dump some of it out? I can have three point four ounces, right? Can you just leave that?"

"Fine." She sighed. She unscrewed the lid and handed it to me, then disappeared behind a partition with the jar dangling from two fingers like it was something that smelled bad. She was gone for an eternity. When she came back, the jar was a quarter full, barely covering my sister's fish body.

"That's three point four ounces? That's nothing!" I yelped, my voice like nails on a metal car door.

Her face was granite.

"I mean, thank you." I took the jar from her hands and screwed the lid on.

"What is it?" she asked. Her face looked sour.

"Um. It's s-serum," I stammered. "Face serum. For my, you know." I gestured toward my face. My sister looked worried. I was not a good liar. "It's organic," I said.

She rolled her eyes once more. "Do not try to bring that through security again. You kids. You can go."

"Okay. Thank you. Merry Christmas," I said through the lump rising fast and hard in my throat. I wouldn't be bringing a jar of organic serum that was actually my sister-ghost-fish through security ever again. I looked at her in her jar, belly pressed against the bottom of the glass. She looked miserable in the tiny pool of water. Her scales were almost completely white now. The security agent slid my tote across the metal table.

"Merry Christmas," she said.

Gabrielle was waiting for me outside security. Her shoes were tied and she'd already stuffed her coat in her carry-on, a suitcase with wheels that was designed to look like a trunk. It was more beautiful than anything I owned.

"What took so long?" she asked. "Is everything okay?"

"Just a long line," I lied. I could feel the tops of my ears turn red.

"Okay," she said, looking at me with a funny expression. I really was such a bad liar. I wanted to explain that I was being haunted by my beautiful sister who was now a fish who liked to swim slow circles around a pickle jar that usually sat on my windowsill. I didn't.

Instead, I sat down and slipped my sneakers on, tied the laces. My throat was stinging like I needed to either sneeze or throw up.

"Coffee," she said as I stood.

"I'll meet you at the gate. Twenty-four, right? I need to put some water on my face or something," I said.

Gabrielle narrowed her eyes.

"Are you okay?" she asked.

"Yes!" I said, too loudly. "I mean, yes, yeah. I'm fine. I'll see you in a second."

I refilled my sister's jar in the water fountain and put her back in the tote bag, whispering "Sorry" until she rolled her eyes, universal sister language for *Please chill out*. I went to the bathroom and sat in a stall, trying to collect myself. I started to hiccup loudly. What was wrong with me? I didn't want to get on the plane. I washed my face in the lukewarm water from the bathroom tap and went to find Gabrielle, who was sitting in front of our gate with her sunglasses on. She looked like she knew everything there was to know about being a person in the world. I wondered what would happen if I left the airport, walked away. I could not show up for work, find an equally mediocre job at an equally mediocre restaurant in the city. I could put my sister's jar back on the windowsill and pretend like none of this had happened.

Once we boarded the plane, I stowed my sister safely in the seat pocket in front of me. I was in the middle seat. I thought about asking Gabrielle to switch so I could look out the window, but I didn't. I pushed the jar deeper into the pocket, then felt bad and pulled it back out so my sister could see the plane.

"What?" Gabrielle asked.

"What?" I replied.

"Why do you keep fidgeting with that jar?"

"I don't know. I'm a nervous flier, I guess," I said.

"Merry Christmas, by the way," she said. "I keep forgetting it's a holiday."

She took a bite of the bagel she'd gotten from the Dunkin' Donuts in the terminal before we boarded the plane and wrinkled her nose.

"I got you a gift," she said. "But I forgot it at home."

"This trip is a gift," I said. I hadn't thought to get her anything and my brain cataloged every item in my bag. What could I give Gabrielle that would show her how much she meant to me? I cringed.

"The trip is free for both of us, basically," Gabrielle said, as if she could read my anxious mind. "We don't have to pay for a place to stay or this flight, so don't worry about it." I opened my mouth to protest but Gabrielle said, "Seriously. Don't."

Some emotion that I couldn't quite discern flickered across her face. I felt small and awkward. Could she sense the smallness and sadness of my life rolling off me? Work was such an equalizer. We all wore black, all went to the same bar after our shifts. But she had to know it was obvious that she had some kind of money, that she had more than the rest of us. *How do you have such a nice apartment while the rest of us live like families of mice?* There was no polite way to ask that question, especially now that I knew the answer, kind of.

Almost as soon as the plane lifted off the tarmac, making my stomach swoop and my ears pop, Gabrielle fell asleep again. She slept through Virginia, North Carolina, Georgia, all the way to Key West. She slept like a dead person, like a moving vehicle was a narcotic for her. When I fell asleep on the train or in a car, my head would slowly loll to my chest until I woke myself up with a jump. Gabrielle, though, was beautiful when she was asleep, even in the harsh light of a plane and especially after the pilots dimmed the cabin lights and the sun started to rise above the horizon outside the airplane window, turning the clouds a bruised pinkish purple.

I'd always known she was beautiful, knew it the first time we met; she was like something otherworldly. The closer we grew, the more I noticed her little flaws — the almost imperceptible chip on one of her front teeth, the way she always had a shadow of a unibrow, how she honked with laughter when she was drunk and less aware of herself — but all those things made her seem real and, in turn, more achingly beautiful. I wondered if it was possible for beauty to be contagious. That, perhaps, some of it might rub off on me.

A teacher I had in high school had told us once, in a futile effort to strike inspiration, that the word *flaw* came from an Old Norse word that meant both a flake of snow and a spark of fire. However clichéd it was, I hadn't forgotten it. *Flaw, flake, fire.* All of Gabrielle's little flakes, sparks, made me want to wrap my arms around her shoulders, press my hand against her warm skin as if it were sand, something I could leave an imprint on, even a brief one.

Gabrielle woke up when we were landing and stretched her arms above her head while sliding down in her seat.

"I feel so much better," she said. She rubbed her eyes. "Sorry, I was a bit off this morning, wasn't I?"

I shrugged. "I'm just excited to be here."

She smiled. "Me too."

From her jar in the back of the seat pocket, my sister waved one of her long fins as if she agreed. I took her jar from the pocket before the plane came to a full stop, held her with both hands, already feeling fraught about leaving her behind.

The town of Key West was pastel-colored and quiet on Christmas morning. We wove through the town in an Uber and I craned my neck, looking at the luscious palm trees interrupted by houses painted in bright colors, mostly pink. There were sweeping front porches and the streets were so quiet compared to the city. My sister zigzagged in her jar, which I held in my lap, as we passed a flock of bright green birds perched in a palm tree that was as tall as the enormous houses, taller. We turned onto a block with GRINNELL spelled out in black letters on a street sign and Gabrielle said, "This is it," and pointed to a towering fence painted dark green with lattice at the top.

"You can let us out here," Gabrielle said to the driver. She opened the door almost before the car came to a halt and I slid out behind her. The air was heavy and humid. I felt like I was home, except the blue sky was warm, not lonely, not menacing. Even the air smelled different, clearer.

For a moment, I had a gnawing feeling this was all some kind of long, horrible joke—moving to the city, my sister in my jar, Gabrielle's offer of a vacation. Soon, someone would say, *Gotcha, you fish-toting freak.* None of it was real. Then Gabrielle removed a key chain from her pocket and unlocked a small door I hadn't noticed, and we ducked inside. The wood creaked closed behind us. The latticework, the muggy warmth, all the luscious green, opened up to us, and I felt for a moment like we were a pair of magical somethings flitting about an enchanted tale with a sparkly ending. I started hiccuping again.

"There's a driveway on the other side, but I couldn't remember the code to open the gate," Gabrielle said, but I was only half listening, trying to hold my breath so my hiccups would go away. We took another few steps into the yard and came upon two columns that stood tall like Greek ruins and, behind the monument, the strangest house I had ever laid eyes on.

"I know," Gabrielle said without even looking at me. "My dad is really into Greek mythology, and he calls this his Mount Olympus. Which everyone else who has visited the house finds incredibly obnoxious." She rolled her eyes. It was the single longest sentence she'd spoken to me about her family.

"It's beautiful," I said, and almost meant it.

"Maybe. In a strange way. If you're into mythology. Let's go inside."

I followed her behind the two columns and down a brick path to the front door, or perhaps it was the back. It was hard to tell—the house stood in the middle of the enormous yard. The front half, or the half closer to us, looked purposely unkempt; wild grasses grew tall and gnarled trees loomed like we were in a forest, making the sky seem darker than it was. From the half just beyond came the sound of running water. The side of the house facing us was all glass, and I glimpsed a sparkle out back, the edge of a blue swimming pool.

The house was one sweeping story. Gabrielle unlocked the front door with another key and typed in a code on a pad installed in the wall. Inside, a skylight flooded the room with white light. Four columns stood in a square in the middle, a bizarre centerpiece, and the furniture was all white, upholstered, and expensive. A tall door stood in the left corner of the house, so tall that if I stood on Gabrielle's shoulders, I still wouldn't have been able to fish around on the ledge of the door for a spare key, but the most striking thing about it was its gray ashy wood, which was divided into panels and engraved with images of flowers and animals.

I followed Gabrielle through the Alice in Wonderland door and was relieved when we emerged into a wing of the house that seemed more normal. The ceilings and doors were average height; there was a kitchen with an island and bar stools and a window that overlooked the pool. Somewhere, a central air-conditioning unit was silently pumping out luxuriously cool air.

Gabrielle led me to a spare bedroom off to the side.

"I'm going to put my bathing suit on and go for a swim," Gabrielle said. "But feel free to do whatever. You can take a nap or eat something — there should be food in the fridge — or unpack or come out to the pool."

"Okay," I said. "Thank you. This is great, it's so beautiful here." Words felt clumsy in my mouth. Money, especially visible money, always made me slightly nervous, like I might ruin it somehow — crack a column, stain the white furniture. But it also made things magical and I marveled at what I was sure was a stocked fridge, the smell of lemon cleaner in the air. I put my bag on the enormous bed in my borrowed room. There was a rug on the floor the color of a cornflower with a yellow pattern stitched in it. It looked similar to the rug on Gabrielle's floor in New York. I put my sister on the bedside table before I unpacked.

"How was your flight?" I asked.

She looked ill, carsick maybe.

"Your scales look shiny today," I said. I could taste the hope in my mouth, tried to swallow it down. This trip was for her.

The windows in my bedroom looked out over the pool. Gabrielle was already swimming, precise hands slicing through the water and legs kicking behind her rhythmically. I carried my sister to the window so she could see.

I dug my bathing suit out of my bag, ripped the tags off with my teeth, and tugged it on. I felt sweaty and grimy from the plane ride. The bathroom attached to the room Gabrielle had assigned me was palatial, bigger than my entire room back in New York. I put my zip-lock bag with my toothbrush and sunscreen next to one of the sinks, splashed water on my face and in my armpits, and breathed in deep.

I took another look at the landscape outside of the bedroom, past my sister perched on the windowsill. The pool was narrow and long and tiled in blue. A brick path hugged the borders of the pool, just wide enough for two people to walk past each other, shoulders brushing.

I left my room and went through the sliding glass door in the kitchen and down the stairs to the pool. I sat on the hot brick, legs crisscrossed. The sun was directly above us, and it felt so good to sit beneath it, to feel the tops of my shoulders turn warm and listen to the lap of cool water. The city felt far away already, and almost cartoonish.

Gabrielle did an elegant flip turn, finished her lap, then swam over to me. Her wet hair glimmered in the sun.

"Hey," she said. "I like your suit. Very chic."

"Thanks," I said. She was wearing a light blue bikini with silver, shimmery threads woven into the material. The bathing suit had little ruffles on the straps. She looked like a sea creature, like she belonged in the water.

"Do you want to come in?" she asked.

"That's okay. I don't love swimming."

"Really?" she asked. "I can teach you."

"I know how. I just don't like it." It bothered me that she'd assumed I couldn't swim and I felt a flash of irritation. I didn't resent her for having access to a mansion in Florida, but there was a stark difference in what each of us had. There was so much I didn't know. There was so much she didn't know.

Gabrielle must have sensed the edge in my voice because she didn't push. She kicked off from the wall with her long legs, distorted and endless below the blue water, and did a few backstrokes.

"I'm going to do a couple more laps but feel free to hang out wherever." She gestured with her hand toward three lounge chairs with cheerful yellow-striped cushions. "There's pool towels on the shelf on the deck."

I stood and walked back up the stairs to the deck, stretched out on one of the chairs. I was exhausted. The sun was heavy on my eyelids and there was a salty clean smell coming from the pool, and I was so glad, for once, to be exactly where I was. My sister was safe, still here, in her jar inside, and Gabrielle was in the pool, close enough that I could hear her precise strokes, her legs beating underwater.

❧

I sat up in the lounge chair. My sister was in the pool and it was draining fast. I was scrambling to my feet, yelling her name, telling her to wait. The water in the pool looked frantic, like it was being vacuumed out. I was almost to the edge and then I was tensing my legs, preparing myself to jump in and rescue her, when I sensed a hand on my shoulder, pulling me back.

"Alison? Are you okay?" Gabrielle asked.

I startled, suddenly awake. She was standing over me, her long dark hair dripping on the pavement.

"You were, like, muttering in your sleep," she said.

I forced a laugh. "Weird. I can't believe I slept so hard."

She flopped down on the chair to my left.

"It feels so good to be in the sun," she said. She stretched like a cat waking up from a long sleep. "Do you need anything?" she asked. "Sunscreen, water, book?"

"I'm going to get some water from the kitchen," I said.

"There's bottles in the fridge and cups in one of the cabinets somewhere. I can never remember where everything is." She stretched another mighty stretch. "Could you grab a bottle of water for me?" she asked. "From the fridge. I didn't bring a pickle jar."

"Sure," I said, ignoring her remark about the jar, not sure if it was a joke or a dig. I slid open the door and stepped inside. My skin turned to gooseflesh in the air-conditioning, and I thought I heard something echo on the other side of the house as I closed the door behind me. I opened the fridge and was reaching in to grab a bottle of water when someone said, "Excuse me, may I help you?"

I shrieked and knocked the row of perfectly aligned water bottles over, sending a few to the floor. I slammed the fridge door and spun around. A woman with a head of bright blond hair was standing on the other side of the kitchen island. There was something familiar about her—she was older, and her blond looked like the same shade of L'Oréal my grandmother used to buy from Rite Aid and have me use on her.

"Oh, shit, I'm sorry," I said, my heart beating hard. "Sorry!" I said again, feeling oddly embarrassed for letting a *shit* fly around an adult. I spent so much time around restaurant people, people my own age, I'd forgotten how to act around a mother, or someone who looked like a mother.

"No, I'm sorry, honey," she said. "I didn't know y'all were coming this week. Assuming you're a friend of Gabrielle's and not a water-bottle thief!" She laughed. "My name's Tara. I take care of the house."

"Yeah. I mean, no, I'm not a thief," I said. "I'm Alison. I'm Gabrielle's friend." I did a nervous half wave from across the island, then bent down to pick up the fallen bottles of water.

"Nice to meet you. I'm so glad Gabrielle's visiting; we almost never see her anymore. And she brought a friend, no less! Miracles never cease."

"It's nice to meet you too." I stood in the kitchen, my bare skin, still sticky with sweat, turning shivery in the cold air.

"I'm just finishing up some polishing in the great room and then I'm out of y'all's hair. It is Christmas, after all. I'm sure y'all have something nice planned."

"Okay, thanks so much," I said without knowing exactly why I was thanking her. I walked outside and handed Gabrielle her water bottle as I sat back down.

"There's a woman named Tara in your kitchen."

"Oh, Tara!" she said. "I didn't think she'd be here on Christmas." Her eyebrows knit together. "Sorry. Did she startle you? She takes care of the house," she said, repeating Tara's words.

It hadn't occurred to me until then that a house needed taking care of, like a child with a babysitter.

"I'm going to go say hi," she said and got up from her chair.

I waited to hear the glass sliding door open and close, then peeked around the back of my chair to see Gabrielle hugging Tara despite her wet bathing suit. She left a wet imprint on Tara's shirt but neither of them seemed to notice. Both of their faces shone, animated with happiness, and then, after a moment, became more serious. Gabrielle was talking with her hands like she did at work when she was asking Juan to cover a shift for her or asking Brandon for extra bar mops. I felt nosy, like I was eavesdropping, even though I couldn't hear a word they were saying. I turned around and faced the pool. I sat in the lounge chair stiffly, arms by my sides, wound up and anxious after my weird, hot dream and the conversation with Tara in the kitchen. I curled

GHOST FISH

my toes and released them, trying to expend some energy. After a few minutes, Gabrielle returned.

"I'm so sorry she caught you by surprise!" she said as she sat down and stretched her body out. The sun made her almost instantly languorous, like the New York version of her had already melted away and left this beautiful water girl who seemed a bit mysterious to me.

"God, Tara is the best. I wish that was who I was actually related to."

I stopped flexing my toes and looked at her.

"What do you mean?" I asked carefully. There was an unspoken exactness in our relationship: We'd become close fast, and although nothing in our New York lives was off-limits, everything that had happened before was. She knew about Noah, about my roommates, about how Brandon got on my nerves when he was in micromanager mode. She knew my breakfast sandwich order, how I drank my tea, where and when I went for runs. My sister was the only one who knew me better. And I knew about the hotel guest Gabrielle had slept with over the summer, which broke every single rule of working at the June, how badly she wanted a gallery show, that her favorite flavor of Hal's seltzer water was mango.

What we didn't know: The names of each other's mothers, the names of each other's siblings, or if we had siblings at all, where and when we'd learned to drive, and all the little tragedies that we'd swept into boxes and left in storage units back

185

home for the moths. And, of course, she didn't know about my ghost. The fish that followed me from before to now.

"My dad is—" She sighed. "I don't know. Not that interested in being a dad, I suppose. And my mother isn't well. They don't really spend much time here anymore, almost none, actually, but Tara has been around for ages, since I was a kid and we used to come here for holidays." Gabrielle smiled. "I used to call her my Florida mom. My actual mom hated that."

My own mother hadn't lived long enough to see her daughters make it through middle school. My father had erased himself from the face of the earth. My grandmother was kind and meant well, but she was exhausted by the time we'd moved into her house. My sister and I certainly had nobody like Tara. It was a wonder that Gabrielle and I had anything in common outside of the restaurant. I wondered for the millionth time what she was doing there, why she worked at all, especially if her dad owned the place, but I nodded, waited, hoping she would go on.

"But it's Christmas! Not the day for sad stories," she said. I opened my mouth to protest. I wanted her stories, all of them, especially the sad ones. But I didn't want to answer questions about my family either, so I let her change the subject.

"Should we go out tonight?" she asked.

I nodded, and Gabrielle got a glimmer in her eye, the same one she got before telling me restaurant "goss," as she put it, like Samuel and one of the girls who worked at the front desk were hooking up in the walk-in, the gleam she had when we went to a party a friend of hers was DJing at what turned out to be Elvis Costello's apartment. (Elvis Costello had never shown up.) "I know just the place," she said.

"Even though it's Christmas?" It felt surreal that it was a winter holiday in the hot light, the pool yards away, its blue water winking in the sun.

"People are always on vacation here," she said, shrugging. "It seems like nothing ever really closes. I'm going to go take a nap before, though."

She stood up, humming a song that was familiar, and did a dreamy, slow spin on the way through the sliding door.

I sat, staring at the now-still water in the pool, thinking of a song I heard long ago on a radio in my dad's truck. I was sure I was making it up—I'd been so young when he'd left, how could I possibly remember such a thing?—but still, I knew the song, knew every beat of it. Gabrielle, my friend with a vaguely British accent, a wealthy father, a vacation house full of Greek columns and busts of Greek gods, was humming "Margarita-ville" by Jimmy Buffett.

I could hear Gabrielle talking to Tara again, words I couldn't make out as I sat in the sun, baking like convenience-store cookie dough in a hot oven. I could feel myself turning greasy, sunscreen running in rivulets down my stomach. New York's winter had made me pale and dry-skinned. I felt so much better already beneath the heavy sun. The pool water looked temptingly blue. Once Gabrielle's voice faded and I heard a car door slam and tires crunch down the pebbled driveway, I went inside to get my sister in her jar, my book, my notebook and pen. I felt like my fingers had fire beneath my nails. I wanted to put it all down on paper, the bright color of Tara's hair, the sound of Gabrielle humming. I hadn't written much since my sister died, but lately, I'd been scribbling again.

I spread a towel on the strip of deck around the pool and put my sister's jar beside me. We'd flown from one cusp of the ocean to another and here I was, looking at an artificial body of water.

She looked at the blue water, longing in her sister-ghost-fish eyes.

"I know," I said. I sat on the edge of the pool and slowly dipped my feet in. "Oh my god. It feels so good."

I kicked my heels against the wall of the pool, watching my legs move in slow motion underwater. It was seductive, but I wouldn't go in. I opened my book instead, a poetry anthology, but my eyes wouldn't focus on the words. I closed it, sighed. I hadn't been in the water in almost seven years. I looked over my shoulder at my sister and she gestured toward the pool with her fins. She couldn't, but I could.

"Okay. Fine," I said. I pushed off the concrete deck and into the pool. Underwater, everything was chlorine blue, bright and light. I had forgotten: Under the water was a whole other world, a place without gravity or any immediate problems other than knowing, at some point, I'd need to take another breath.

My sister waved her fins around in her jar when I came up

for air. I wiped water from my eyes. She was so bright in the Florida sun, almost as bright as she'd been in the beginning.

"It's nice, but it still makes me anxious," I said to my sister, trying to keep my voice low. I pushed myself out of the pool, sat next to my sister, and reached for the sunscreen. We sat there in a happy silence and I thought that I hadn't felt so simply *good* in so long; I felt like I was becoming myself, coming back to someone I used to love. I hugged my legs to my chest and rested my forehead on my knees, looking down into the cave of my own body. The backs of my knees started to sweat and I unfurled.

"So," I said. I wished so badly I could hear her voice, not in a dream but in real life. I wished she could tell me what she wanted, what she was feeling. What if I was making a mistake?

"What if we're making a mistake?" I said out loud.

She shook her head. *No.* I nodded. My eyes burned from the pool water and I hiccuped again, just once.

When we went back inside, I could hear Gabrielle moving around her room, the clatter of clothes on wooden hangers. I showered and put on a long-sleeved black dress and my new sandals, then went to sit in the kitchen and wait. I could hear her unzipping things, a bottle of foundation or perfume against a sink counter, the soft hum of music. Getting-ready sounds. She came out in a pale yellow dress that looked silky and light brown sandals that almost matched her sun-darkened calves, making her look barefoot.

"I love that dress," I said.

She smiled. "Do you think you're going to be hot in long sleeves?" she asked. "I know it's December, but it's so humid."

I shrugged. "I'll be fine."

"Wait," she said. "I have something that I was just thinking would look better on you than me."

She walked back into her room. I could see her from my perch at the kitchen island as she dumped whatever was still in her suitcase directly onto the floor. I could feel myself smiling alone in the kitchen and realized I was smiling at the fact of Gabrielle in her room thinking of something that would look nice on me. She dug through the pile and unearthed a dress that was almost but not quite white, like a linen curtain.

"Voilà," she said, walking back into the kitchen. "For you."

I didn't hesitate to accept this time. I wanted her generosity. And the dress was gorgeous. I peeled off my long-sleeved dress that did already feel too hot and pulled the white one over my head. It floated down around me until the thin straps rested on my shoulders. The hem fell right in the middle of my calves. I'd never thought to buy a long dress like this one, but it was so comfortable and floaty, thin and lovely with a low back that left the curve of my spine exposed.

I left my black dress on the kitchen floor like a discarded skin and said, "Wow. I love it. I'm getting married in this dress."

Gabrielle considered me from across the kitchen. "You kind of look like Emily Dickinson. The signature white dress."

"That is the nicest thing you've ever said to me."

Gabrielle laughed and told me to sit still. My hair was wavy around my face and she walked behind me and braided my hair with quick fingers. When she was finished, she put her warm, soft hands on my shoulder.

"Perfect," she said.

I crossed my arms. I had goose bumps I didn't want her to see.

"We can walk from here," she said, and we went through the backyard and down the brick path to the road. It was quiet and the sun was going down, making the night sky bloom indigo. I could hear frogs croaking, a throaty chorus, from the vegetation at the sides of the road. The street was quiet and we walked down the middle of it, one of us on either side of the yellow line.

"Where are we going?" I asked.

"There's a big bar on Duval that always has a band playing. It's kind of famous around here, for tourists, at least. It's fun. It was the first place I drank a beer outside of my house," she said. Florida made her nostalgic, it seemed. I tucked this fact away like a treasure.

"Did you... grow up here?" I asked.

"No, we only came on holidays," Gabrielle said, and grimaced. "I know how that sounds. It's exactly how it sounds. We're the rich people that are ruining yet another pretty place. But I love it here — it feels like home, for some reason."

I kept my face very still, hoping she'd continue.

"My dad grew up in Cuba," Gabrielle said after a moment.

"And my mom is from the UK. I was born there, but we moved to Manhattan when I was really young. That didn't take, so they packed up and moved to LA after a few years, but I was in boarding school in Virginia by then."

This, too, was new information. "Boarding school? What was that like?" My knowledge of boarding school consisted of a childhood obsession with Harry Potter and the military academy at the very edge of the town I grew up in where misbehaving boys were sent. We only ever saw them at church and sometimes Walmart, where they always looked homesick and tired.

"I loved it, actually," she said. "Staying in the same place, seeing the same people every day. And there was an art teacher, Josie. I adored her." I listened to the twin slap of our sandals on the pavement. "She told me about Alice Neel and Celia Paul and using big gobs of paint instead of just keeping tight charcoal sketches in a notebook."

"And you went to college after? In New York?"

"In Ithaca—it's three hours or so from the city. Cornell. But it didn't work out, obviously."

"Cornell," I said. "Wow."

"Yeah, except my dad stopped paying my tuition. I told him I was studying business and when he found out I was doing art, he gave me an ultimatum: Change my major or he'd cut me off. I didn't think it was worth taking out student loans to pay for it myself, so I dropped out and moved to the city," she said. Her lips twisted. "I know, poor rich girl. And truthfully, I think maybe I did just want to be in the city doing something real, or—I don't know. Whatever." She shrugged. "I could have asked my mom for the money but she was so sick then. So I paint on my own and I work at the June and maybe it's just better this way."

"Poor rich girl," I said, but I wrapped an arm around her shoulder and put a teasing lilt in my voice so she'd know I was kidding. Kidding, but only halfway. I was envious and a bit afraid of my envy. I didn't want it to strangle our friendship. If I had known all of this, Cornell and boarding school, rich parents, I would never have considered us capable of a friendship. I wondered, for the millionth time since Juan's revelation, why she worked at her dad's hotel, especially if he had cut her off.

"You're like an alien," I said. "Someone from another planet."

She kissed me on the cheek with a big, comic smack and we walked wound up in each other, her arm around my neck, mine around her waist. My hand felt enormous on her and it felt good, like I could keep her safe if she needed me. The sun had gone all the way down and the night enveloped us. We walked toward the sidewalk as the little downtown area of Key West came into view. I could hear music drifting toward us.

"Where did you go to college?" Gabrielle asked.

"I didn't," I said, then pointed to the sky. "Look! The moon!"

Gabrielle laughed and it was her turn to let me change the subject.

"You really did need a break from the city," she said.

"Is your mom better now?" I asked.

"She's okay." Her voice was flat. She changed the subject to the drink she couldn't wait to order at Sloppy Joe's, something blue and frozen. I laughed. I couldn't imagine her drinking anything other than tequila or a red wine with a name I couldn't pronounce. I was glad she was also a person who drank terrible frozen drinks.

We walked a few more blocks into the town and stopped at a little restaurant for fried oysters and French fries and cold beers.

"I feel like a fisherman," Gabrielle said.

I licked my lips. I was happy, in all-capital handwritten letters. HAPPY in a plain, easy, fried-food-and-cheap-beer way. We threw out our trash and walked to a bar that stretched half a block, the words SLOPPY JOE'S BAR outlined in red neon that buzzed like mosquitoes. The awning above the door read *Cocktails, Piña Coladas, Sloppy Joe's Specials* in cursive. I could hear the twang of a guitar screeching from inside.

A small group stood on the sidewalk under the awning, chatting and smoking, women with sunburned backs and tropical-fruit-printed dresses, men in plaid shirts and baseball caps. Gabrielle bummed a cigarette from one of the women and we split it, smoking quickly. Once we were done, buzzing like the mosquitoes darting in and out of the neon light, we walked inside. Gabrielle bought us frozen drinks in tall cups with straws in the shape of squiggles. A guy in a cowboy hat and blue jeans sitting at the other end of the bar sent us tequila shots and tipped his hat at us when we waved and mouthed *Thanks*. We took the shots and disappeared ourselves onto the dance floor, laughing so hard our eyes teared up. A band called the Dirty Senators was playing songs about love and summer and answers and salvation and heads on shoulders, and I danced until sweat dripped down my back, doing my best not to think about my sister, alone in her jar in an unfamiliar house.

When we got back to the house that night, we did a number on the kitchen. We drank water directly from the tap and made snacks that only someone who spent the evening dancing and drinking frozen drinks would crave: plain crackers covered in cheese, melted in the microwave, sour cream plunked on top; toast with cinnamon and sugar piled on; a bag of microwave popcorn; more melted cheese. Our laughter echoed through the big house. We polished off the popcorn and my eyes felt tired. The clock on the microwave read 3:49 in its green, unwavering digits.

"So what was up with that jar?" Gabrielle asked. I blinked. The morning before, the airport, felt like another lifetime, like years and years had passed since then.

"I told you," I said, forcing my voice to come out even and normal, "it was just a water bottle. You know, like reduce-reuse-recycle."

Gabrielle laughed, but it sounded mean. Or maybe I was being sensitive. Or something halfway between.

"Then why were you nodding at it? And keeping it in your tote bag with a hand on it like it was a baby or something? I was getting worried about you, honestly."

Her tone was sardonic, almost, which stung. I hadn't prodded at her perfect-little-rich-girl life or the weird marble busts in the big room we'd walked through when we arrived and had avoided since. I fidgeted with the edge of the plate we'd eaten the gooey, melted cheese and crackers from, grease pooling in the center.

"Why do you care?" I asked. I could hear the defensiveness in my voice.

"Okay, okay," Gabrielle said. "Fine, sorry, bringing a glass pickle jar full of dirty water on vacation is definitely not weird."

I knew she was trying to bring some levity into a room that was now tense, but I wasn't in the mood. She didn't understand because I couldn't tell her. It was impossible—impossible to explain any of it because I wasn't sure what was real myself. Was I haunted or was my brain permanently damaged by my sister's drowning, dying? Was it all imagined? I knew it wasn't. I was pretty sure it wasn't, but I knew that's what Gabrielle would think and I could not bear that, not being believed. My sister not being believed.

"I'm going to bed," I said and started picking up our empty plates and putting them in the sink. "I'll clean this up in the morning."

"Tara will get it."

I wanted to grab her by the wrists and shake some of my

life into her. *Tara will get it!* Tara, her maid! I crossed the room, let the plate in my hand drop hard into the sink, said, "Night," and walked to the bedroom that Gabrielle had told me was mine. I could feel her eyes on my back as I gently closed the door behind me, making a point not to slam it that was more petty than restrained. I was being strange and edgy, and it wasn't her fault I was feeling so irritated, but I was tired of having secrets.

I took off the dress I'd borrowed from Gabrielle and carefully hung it on a wooden hanger in the empty closet. I stared at it, hanging there alone. It probably cost more than my rent, I thought with a little bit of anger and a little bit of jealousy. I took it off the hanger and dropped it on the floor.

I turned and walked to my sister, who was still on the windowsill.

"Now do you get it? You can't leave me alone here." I hated the sound of my voice, all whiny and insistent. Her fish eyes looked sad in the jar, or scared. Her fins and her long delicate tail drifted, pale, aimless.

"We went dancing tonight." I sighed and carried her to the little wooden bedside table. I set her down and sat on the still-made bed, crisp like a hotel's, Tara's handiwork I was sure. "I hate doing things that you like without you. I promised I'd take you to the ocean. Tomorrow, maybe." She swam an excited loop in her jar and it made me angry that she was so happy to go away. I stood up and walked into the bathroom, flipped on the light, and stared at the sunburned girl in the mirror. I wanted to like her but she looked so distant. My eyes were so far away and my lips were peeling from the sun. I shut the lights off and washed my face in the dark.

"Are you even going to miss me?" I asked my sister when I got into bed. We were lying in the dark but the moon was so full, it leaked enough light into the room that I could see her shoot to the top of her jar and bob up and down indignantly, like *Yes, obviously, how dare you even ask me that.*

"I'm sorry," I said. I bit my lip. The back of my throat burned. "I'm so, so sorry."

For what? I wanted her to ask. *For everything,* I would have replied. But she moved her fins from side to side reassuringly, like someone waving a hand to dismiss an unnecessary thought. She understood me and I understood her; of course she would miss me. Of course. If it were possible to stay, she would. But what was possible was for me to let her go and be okay, and she was trusting me to grasp that.

"Okay," I whispered. She nodded and it felt like a circle had been drawn around us. Nothing could take away what we were to each other, not the ocean, not dying, not anyone else. I fell asleep like that, understanding slipping over me like a lullaby.

⌒ٯ⌒

I'd always liked the sound of plates clattering together, the soundtrack to a dinner that's winding down—a mom and dad peeled from a sitcom, cleaning up the table, or busboys banging up and down stairs with dish bins, the familiar chaos of a restaurant kitchen just beginning service.

When I was young, I liked to walk around our cul-de-sac at dinnertime when the light was just starting to leak from the sky. If it was quiet and not too hot to leave the windows open, I would be able to hear the sound of dinner being cleaned up, the echo of plate on plate. So when I woke up to the sound of plates being stacked together, cabinet doors closing with their full thunks, silverware jingling into the correct drawers, I thought for a minute that I was home. Not New York home, but Awnor home. I was waking up on my narrow bed, my sister still sleeping in the twin next to mine. I could hear my grandmother in the kitchen, boiling water to make the instant coffee she swore she liked better than the brewed stuff.

I blinked at my sister, asleep in her jar next to me. There was a new stillness inside me. I should—I could—let her go. But first I needed to apologize to Gabrielle for the night before. It suddenly seemed so silly—Gabrielle and I had so much time ahead of us to work it all out. My phone was under the pillow on the empty side of my bed and I picked it up. It was 12:04. I couldn't remember the last morning I'd slept until noon. Possibly never? I got out of bed and put on a pair of denim shorts that had once been a pair of my mom's jeans and a dark green T-shirt, whispered good morning to my sister, and walked into the kitchen. Tara was cleaning up the mess we'd made the night before.

"Good morning, Sleeping Beauty," she said in a jolly tone.

I'd never thought of someone as *jolly* before, but Tara fit the word. She had red cheeks, that thick, blond hair, and a big smile accentuated with cherry-red lipstick. She was also wearing denim cutoffs and a green T-shirt.

"Ha, look!" she said. "We're twins!"

"Ha-ha," I forced out. "Can I help clean up? I'm sorry we made a mess."

"Sweet pea, this is my bread and butter. Sit down. What do you want for breakfast?"

"I'm okay, thank you."

"Bacon and toast?"

"Really, I'm fine."

"I'll make some just in case, and if you get hungry, it's there."

"Okay," I said, sensing that this was a losing battle. "Thanks."

She turned on the stove and pulled out a frying pan. It almost sparkled, something I assumed was her handiwork.

"Have you seen Gabrielle?" I asked.

"Sure have, she was up early, all bright-eyed and bushy-tailed, and swam. That girl loves the water. She's like a fish. Oh! She left you a note." Tara slid a folded-up piece of paper across the kitchen island. "Sorry," she said, "I got a smidge of grease on it."

> alison—
> went to town to shop etc.

text me if you need anything.

beach later?

xx g

PS sorry about the jar thing. hope you're feeling okay.

Tara turned away, letting me read the note without her eyes on me. I didn't need anything. I did want to go to the beach. I sat at the counter as Tara deftly cooked some bacon, fried a couple of eggs, toasted bread, all at the same time. It was as if she had two extra arms. I put the note on the island in front of me and smoothed the piece of paper out, absentmindedly trying to disappear the creases where it had been folded.

"So, tell me everything. Where are you from?" Tara asked.

I was surprised by the question and opened my mouth to speak but inhaled too quickly. My breath hiccuped in my throat and I started coughing, tears gathering at the corners of my eyes.

"Lord Almighty," Tara said. She filled a glass with water and handed it to me. "Breathe, girl."

I drank a sip, tried to gather myself. "Sorry," I said, laughing now. "I came here from New York with Gabrielle."

"But you're not from New York," Tara said. She wasn't asking.

"No, I'm from a small town. Closer to here than there, actually."

"Mysterious," she said. "I like it. And I figured. I can hear it in your voice. Carolinas?" she asked. "Georgia?"

"Yes," I said without specifying. I was still enjoying being a rootless flower, clipped from a branch and placed in a vase. I didn't want to change that just yet. I instinctively liked Tara but I knew that anything I told her would likely reach Gabrielle's ears. I was glad, for now at least, that Gabrielle knew only the version of me that wasn't a history of death-death-death.

Tara flipped the eggs without using a spatula, just the handle of the frying pan and an expert flick of her wrist.

"Is this your only job?" I asked. It sounded rude after I said it, but I was curious.

"No. I'm a musician too. If you can believe that. I play the guitar in this little band."

"Really?" I asked. "That's so cool."

"Yes, ma'am," she said, and winked. She had blue eyeshadow dabbed on her lids, and I could see why Gabrielle loved Tara so much. She was alive.

"My mom taught me how to play the banjo, of all things, when I was a girl and then I taught myself how to play piano on the old clunker at school," she continued. "I've been hooked ever since."

I didn't miss my mom very often. It wasn't that I hadn't loved her or that I was particularly unfeeling. She had just been gone for so long, since I was so young. I could watch movies about daughters and their mothers without flinching, so feeling a flicker of jealousy imagining Tara learning how to play banjo from her mom surprised me.

"Does she live nearby? Your mom?" I asked.

Tara slid bacon and eggs in front of me. They smelled good, nostalgic, and my stomach growled.

"She died a few years ago," Tara said. She said it simply, plainly. It was a fact.

"I'm so sorry, Tara," I said. I looked down at my plate.

"Y'all should come to Mallory Square tonight. We're playing a little gig."

"Okay. That sounds fun," I said. I meant it. I liked Tara. I was flickering with jealousy — she reminded me a little of my mother, her sense of humor and her blue eyeshadow. But I still wanted to see her play a banjo in a square.

"Around sunset," she said. We talked a little more as I ate, and before I realized it, I'd devoured two eggs and what seemed like half a pound of bacon. Tara lifted the now-empty plate, rinsed it in the sink, and put it in the dishwasher, which she kicked shut with a foot clad in a purple Skechers sneaker and turned on.

"Thank you so much," I said. "That was delicious. And thank you for cleaning up."

"Don't mention it, honey," she said. She swiped at the kitchen counter once more with a sponge, then brushed her palms against her thighs.

"All right, I'm ready to blow this Popsicle stand. I'll see you at sunset, sweet pea."

"Yes, ma'am," I said, startling myself with a phrase I hadn't used in years.

"Good manners," she said and winked again. Without giving me a second to reply, she was gone.

When my sister and I were younger, my mom would put us in dresses and bows for school. My sister would take her bow off the moment we left the house to walk to school, zip it up in her lunch box. She found no value in rules she couldn't understand, such as having to wear a pretty, useless bow in her hair. I would command her to put it back on with all the force of an older sister, terrified our mother would find out we weren't following her rules, and she would ignore me until my big-sister bluster finally got under her skin. She loved to deliver a sharp pinch in retaliation, and on a bad day, we would devolve into a silent scratching, biting, all-out fight before we even got to the end of the block. But when school was over, we would skip home hand in hand, the fight forgotten, sometimes stopping to pick dandelions or catch lizards in one of the empty lots in our neighborhood.

There was no one else in my life I was capable of raging against and loving with such ferocity. It made me feel raw. *She* made me feel raw. Now, as I sat on the bed and watched her drift around in her jar, I asked for the three hundredth time why she'd come back to me. My sister rolled her eyes as if she were eleven and sixteen and twenty-one and eight all at once. There was a lot we hadn't gotten to talk about, but I knew she was rolling her eyes at a question that didn't really matter. What mattered was that she'd come back. But now, she was leaving all over again. I didn't know, still, what I would have done without her those first feral months of my new life.

"So. The ocean," I said.

She nodded her fish head. She was still on my bedside table.

"I just, like, unscrew your lid and dump you in?"

She nodded.

"And then what?"

She mimed swimming with her fins.

"Swim after you?"

She shook her head no.

"Swim away from you?"

She shook her head yes, slowly.

"What if I don't want to go back to New York?" I asked, though I knew that wasn't a question she could answer with a shake of her delicate head.

Something twisted in my stomach. I was disappointed that I hadn't become the kind of person who loved New York. But I'd spent six months living with my sister-ghost-fish, and now that I was back down south and on the precipice of being alone again, I knew loving the city was an act of pretend. I had moved to the city to become something, to use a shiny place and new people to prop myself up for a little while, but now I was okay. I was no longer afraid of empty rooms.

I wondered, for the first time in a while, what my mom would have thought about all this. She loved having two girls so close in age. I could picture her sitting on my grandmother's

tiny front porch, barefoot, smiling at the thought of us defy-
ing the laws of physics, the laws of living, whatever it was
that brought us together. I thought about my mother and my
grandmother and my sister, the ribbon running through us all.
I missed them. I missed my sister and she was sitting in her jar
right in front of me.

Something clanked in the kitchen and we both flinched,
she in her jar and me cross-legged on a bed that technically
belonged to a wealthy man whose name I didn't know. We
were both jumpy, my sister and I. I stood up and she nodded
her head like everything would be okay, like she was resting
her case. I nodded back. I knew she was right.

I'll be right back, I mouthed to her, then walked into the
kitchen.

Between sitting in the kitchen talking to Tara and sitting in
my bedroom talking to my sister, I had almost forgotten about
my weird spat with Gabrielle the night before. She was standing in front of the kitchen sink, looking gloomy despite the sun
spilling through the windows.

"Hey," I said, sitting on a bar stool at the island. "What
have you been up to?"

"Just running a few errands."

I cleared my throat. "I'm sorry about last night. I was being
weird, I know. I think the day just caught up with me."

"No, I'm sorry, I drank too much. I was only trying to be
funny."

"Let's forget it," I said. "Let's go to the beach."

"I was hoping you would say that," Gabrielle replied.

I moved to get up and go back to my room to change into my bathing suit but Gabrielle said, "So. I hope this isn't strange."

"What?" I asked. I couldn't imagine how this day, my life as a whole, could get much stranger.

"My dad owns the hotel on the edge of town," she began.

I tried to keep my face from rearranging itself at the idea of her dad owning another hotel, but she noticed.

"I know, sorry, I know that's insane."

"Don't apologize," I said. "It's cool. My very own London Tipton."

"Ha, you can explain who that is later. Anyway, the hotel has a private beach and I thought maybe we could go there? Just so we don't have to worry about packing chairs and finding parking." She seemed nervous again, like she was when she'd first invited me to Florida. I couldn't help smiling at her. "What?" she said. "We don't have to. We can go to one of the parks or hang out here instead."

"Let's go to the fancy beach," I said. "I'd *love* to go to the fancy beach. I'll put my bathing suit on."

Back in my room, I mouthed *I'm sorry* to my sister in her jar. I couldn't return her to the ocean at a private beach with rich people flouncing around. It wouldn't be right. It needed to be just us. She bobbed up and down, agreeing. "Thank you," I whispered.

I returned to the kitchen. Gabrielle was spinning around

the house like a tropical storm, putting water bottles and towels and sunscreen in a tote bag, debating which book she should bring, asking me three times if I was sure I didn't want her to bring a magazine for me.

"Gabrielle, it's just the beach. If I get bored I'll go for a walk or something. If we both get bored we can leave."

"That's true, I guess," she said, as if the idea of going somewhere without being fully prepared never occurred to her. I thought of her suitcase, trunk-size. She narrowed her eyes as if visualizing a to-do list.

"Okay, you're right," she finally said. "Let's go."

She lifted a set of keys from a hook in the kitchen I hadn't noticed until just now. I followed her through the backyard, down the brick path that wound around the columns. She pressed a button, and the fence rolled open and we walked halfway down the block and stopped in front of a forest-green Jeep.

"We can take this," she said, pressing a button on the key fob that made the car chirp twice. "My dad doesn't like having cars in the driveway. He says it ruins the ambience." She raised her eyebrows.

I was so thrilled to climb into a Jeep with the top down that I didn't even care how obnoxious this was, the idea of ruining expensive ambience with an expensive car.

We drove through Key West, passing pastel-colored B and Bs that looked like bright, tropical gingerbread houses with porches on all three floors, butterflies landing on white picket fences, palm trees tangled with kudzu. The sun was at the very top of the sky, dripping all over us like honey, its warmth sticky. Gabrielle got on the highway and just as quickly got off, turned down a long driveway that ended at a black wrought-iron gate. Beyond the gate was a hotel that looked like a castle except for the fact that it was pink. The gate opened as her car approached—we didn't even have to stop—and Gabrielle guided the Jeep around the circular driveway, parked it in front of the hotel, and left her keys in the ignition. I felt like I was in a commercial for expensive perfume or bottled water.

We had to walk through the hotel lobby to get to the beach. It smelled like money—literally, like fresh, clean paper. The thwack of our flip-flops against the marble floor echoed and I tried not to feel out of place. It was beautiful. It was all so beautiful. And I was happy to be walking through a fancy hotel lobby on my own vacation instead of working in one for a change.

The beach was lovely, perfect. White sand and palm trees that curved in Ls with hammocks strung between, lounge chairs with plush pink-and-white-striped cushions protected from the sun by matching pink-and-white-striped umbrellas. The water was cerulean and irresistible, and I was with Gabrielle, a person I knew would never let me drown. I sat on the shore and watched her float on her back, and for the first time since my sister died, the ocean didn't scare me. The water held Gabrielle so perfectly and I wanted to float beside her, watch the water bead on my stomach. I walked in until I was ankle deep, and the Earth did not stop spinning; I was not immediately swept out into the depths. I waded farther, to my knees, hips, until I reached Gabrielle and then I was floating too, just fingertips away from her. She put her feet on the sandy ground and put her arms underneath me. My muscles clenched and I felt myself start to sink.

"Relax," she said. "You're above water. You don't need to hold your breath. The salt will buoy you."

Her lips looked red under the sun and against the blue water. I wanted to reach up and touch them, her lips. After a moment, she let go, and nothing bad happened. The ocean didn't turn into a raging froth. I felt muscles in my back relax, muscles that had been tensed for so long I had forgotten what it was like to let go. The sky above me looked like the ending of a happy movie.

We floated on our backs, gossiped about Juan and Mike and Brandon and the rest of the cast of characters at the June, which seemed, now, like it existed in another world.

"Oh," I said after we got out and unfolded ourselves onto two of the lounge chairs arranged artfully in the sand, letting the sun evaporate the water left on our skin from our swim. "I saw Tara this morning and she invited us to see her play her banjo. I said we'd go. I think she said it was at Mallory Park?"

Gabrielle snorted. "Mallory Square. She is ridiculous. That was nice of you."

"I want to. I think it's cool," I said. Gabrielle's nose crinkled below her dark sunglasses and I couldn't see her eyes.

"Or, I don't know. But it sounds fun. I like her. We talked for a while this morning. She reminds me of—of someone."

"If you want to…" Gabrielle said. I was surprised by her reluctance; she was normally up for anything. Plus she seemed to love Tara.

"We can go!" Gabrielle said, noticing my surprise, I think. "We should go. Mallory Square is pretty at sunset. A little touristy, but so is the rest of this town, I guess."

"I mean, we don't have to," I said. "If you have something else planned."

Gabrielle yawned and stretched out on her chair. "No, no, that's fine. I'd like to lie here for an hour or so, then we can go home and shower before. Are you hungry yet?"

I was hungry. We wrapped the hotel's pink-and-white-striped towels around our waists and walked to the pool bar for burgers and fries. Gabrielle's wet hair stuck to her shoulders as she ate her burger in five enormous bites. We looked at her empty plate and laughed and it felt weird to eat a burger with a pink middle under the sun, so I gave her half of mine, which she also devoured, and I loved her appetite, the way she filled herself when she was hungry. The way she knew her wants, could point to them, then swallow them whole.

Later we went for a walk. The beach in Key West, beyond the hotel, was more rugged than the manicured strip of ocean-front where guys who were about my age in pink polo shirts raked the sand back into place anytime it was disturbed. The water was more gray than blue. As we walked away from the hotel, I noticed rocks stuck in the sand here and there, and we drew closer to jagged, splintered pilings jutting out of the water. It looked like a dock had burned away and the pilings had been snapped like toothpicks.

"What's that?" I asked Gabrielle, pointing at the broken wood.

She shrugged. "Hurricane, I guess. I'm surprised they haven't fixed it yet. My dad would be so annoyed."

The blackened tips of the pilings looked so violent. It was just something broken, decaying in the salt water, but it surprised me how callow, or maybe callous, Gabrielle could be. Destruction, an annoyance. I wondered if I'd felt safe swimming in this ocean because it was the ocean of rich, fancy hotel people. I felt a pang of guilt, like I shouldn't be enjoying this while my sister was home. Like I was betraying my mother and grandmother by going beyond gates they would never have dreamed of opening for them. Gabrielle bent down and picked up a piece of bright red glass made almost completely opaque by months or years of being worn down by sand and sea.

"It's the color of blood," Gabrielle said. "Fake blood." She laughed. "Like a vampire sucking someone's neck."

She handed the piece of glass to me and I carried it back to our bags, which we had left, unguarded, on our chairs. Nobody had stolen our wallets or moved our towels. I wondered what it was like, to always expect safety. I put the piece of glass into my bag and kept reaching inside it to run my fingers around the edges on the quiet ride home.

❧

Mallory Square was a plaza on the water, and Gabrielle was right, it was a hive of tourists taking photos of everything, vendors selling key chains and mini–novelty license plates. We had walked from Gabrielle's house, and as we drew closer to the water, the streets got more and more crowded. We crossed beneath the gate, WELCOME TO MALLORY SQUARE MARKET painted in blue script on a white sign that curved above us, reminiscent of an old-timey circus poster.

Gabrielle hooked her elbow through mine. It wasn't quite sunset yet, the sky still clinging to its blue. At a bar in the middle of the square we purchased cold beers in plastic cups that immediately started sweating in our hands and joined the rest of the crowd milling about. There was a person painted silver and standing very still on top of a mop bucket as if he were a statue. There was a man dressed as a pirate, a parrot on one arm and a snake wrapped around the other. There were tables selling temporary tattoos and jewelry made from sea glass and watercolors of the very square we were standing in.

We found Tara under a green-canopied tailgate tent. I had half expected her to be dressed in jewels and scarves, purple fringe and glitter, but she was wearing the same denim shorts and green T-shirt she'd had on earlier when we'd accidentally matched. A couple of plastic boxes full of cords and musical gear sat beneath the tent.

"Hi, Tara," we said, waving.

"No beer for your auntie Tara?" she asked, laughing as she squeezed Gabrielle into a hug and kissed both sides of her face, leaving soft smears of lipstick behind. She gave me a tight hug too, then introduced us to her friend Nancy, the lead singer. The sky was starting to dissolve into a misty pink.

"You've got quite the crowd," Gabrielle said to Tara, and I couldn't tell if she was being sarcastic or not. The square was packed, but nobody seemed to be there to hear a banjo player and her lead singer, Nancy. Tara waved her off.

"Go get me a margarita, Gabi. Alison and I have work to do." She pointed at a box. "Want to be our merch girl?" she asked me. I nodded and helped her and Nancy unpack a microphone and cords, unfolded a folding table, and laid out shirts that read THE SCREAMING ALLIGATORS.

"Great band name," I said. We had set the table up to the right of the tent and Tara and I sat in metal chairs, folding and arranging the T-shirts by size.

"Thanks. My son came up with it," Tara said.

"You have a son?" I asked.

"Yep. Joe. He's a sweetheart. About your age, probably. His dad and I put him through hell when he was young but he turned out okay. He's a really good kid. I'm lucky."

I ran my finger over the sharp crease I'd just made in one of the now perfectly folded green T-shirts.

"What about you?" Tara asked. "Where's your family?"

"I don't really have family," I said. It was unlike me to be so forthcoming. I usually made a joke or changed the subject when the topic of family came up, but in the middle of that busy square, I wanted to tell Tara all of it; I felt like I could share every horrible thing that had ever happened to me and she would make it seem okay. She would make me feel like I could still have a life, even after the worst thing I could ever imagine happening had happened, was happening again. I was starting to realize that maybe I didn't think I deserved a full life, an easy life, a life like anyone else's. Maybe that was why I'd moved to New York in the first place: New York, especially when you were new and all alone, was most definitely not easy. My tiny room, my tiny paycheck, fit tidily into my tiny life. If I made myself as small as possible, whatever had taken my mom and my sister wouldn't find me.

Tara was looking at me, waiting.

"I had a sister," I began. "I had a mom, and a grandmother. They all died. Can you believe that?" I asked, the words tumbling out of my mouth now. "If I tried to write a book about it, nobody would believe it. But they're all gone."

"Oh, Alison," Tara said. "I am so sorry."

I stretched my arms above my head, toward the sky. It felt lovely to have Tara, whose mother had taught her how to play the banjo, whose son had named her band, make a face of love and sorrow at me. It was so rare that I was ever around a mother. I leaned back, and my chair hit Gabrielle's thighs.

"Ow," she said, although I had barely grazed her. I hadn't realized she'd returned already with a margarita for Tara. I wondered what she'd heard, and I guessed most of it, by the look on her face.

"Sorry," I said, looking up at her.

"Here you go," Gabrielle said, passing the icy plastic cup to Tara. She licked the condensation off her fingers and I closed my eyes for a moment. There were goose bumps on my arms but the backs of my thighs were sweaty. I felt hot and cold at the same time.

"Thanks, baby doll," she said and took a big sip from the plastic cup. "What do y'all have planned for the rest of the night?"

"Dinner at the crab shack," said Gabrielle. "Want to come?"

"Would love to, but Nancy and I have big plans. Bingo at the Lutheran church," she said cheerfully. "We should probably get started here before the sun goes down."

Tara and Nancy finished getting set up, then played a cover of a Rhiannon Giddens song. It didn't take long for a small crowd to gather at their makeshift stage, their green tent. They were good—better than good. Tara's fingers flew over the banjo and Nancy's voice was husky and textured. But I was having a hard time focusing on their music. Gabrielle was quiet, and her face looked drawn. She stared straight ahead as if her eyes were glued to Tara and Nancy, which was strange, since she hadn't seemed excited about coming.

"I love Rhiannon Giddens," I said.

"Mhmm," Gabrielle replied.

There was something hard and closed off in the space between us, and she wouldn't make eye contact with me. I waited a few songs, then couldn't help myself. "Are you... mad? Or something?" I asked.

Gabrielle stepped to the front of the crowd, stuffed a few

bills in their tip jar, then walked toward the water. I followed, almost running to keep up with her long strides.

The railing by the water was thronged with tourists, but Gabrielle found a small opening to lean against as we watched the last of the sunset. The sky was a furious orange, the top of the sun outlined a bright, unreal red as it sank low and lower.

"I didn't know about your family," Gabrielle said. Her voice was quiet.

"What?" I asked, although I knew she'd overheard my conversation with Tara. I knew exactly what. We were both facing the water, the sun sinking over the ocean. She turned to face me but I kept my eyes trained on the horizon.

"It's so strange," Gabrielle finally said, breaking the tense silence. "I've never had a friend like you, someone who doesn't...bother me. I've always needed so much space from other people, space to paint and think, but not from you. I know you don't want to talk about where you came from and that's fine, I don't really care to think about the past much either. I thought we both just had shit we didn't want to talk about, but you've known Tara for a day and you're already telling her everything about yourself." She exhaled, one hard, long breath. "I'm not angry, I just..." She stopped. "Are you someone I can trust? Or maybe it feels like you don't trust me. And you have that jar. I know you, I know it means something, but you won't say what."

"So you're upset with me because of a *jar*?" I asked. "That's all it takes?"

I knew I was being mean. It wasn't just a jar, it was my entire life, my ghost. I was dodging her question and I knew it. I felt sweaty and dirty and undone, like I would have no problem taking a tire iron to a car's headlights. I looked at my hands, clutching the black railing separating us from the water below. There was dirt under my fingernails. It hadn't occurred to me that Gabrielle was jealous that I had confided in Tara, confided in someone who was not her, and everything felt impossible. I didn't know how to untangle it. It didn't seem like it would be worth it, telling her this crazy, impossible-to-understand secret. But I couldn't keep doing this, keep acting like what she could see, what she felt, wasn't true.

Gabrielle didn't reply. She stared at the water, a sad look on her face.

"Fine," I said finally. "Come with me."

I walked off to a little alley between two brick storefronts, a shop full of knickknacks and a shop full of Cuban cigars that smelled earthy and herby. She followed me to the back of the alley. It was dark. I didn't want anyone to overhear me. I turned to her.

"My mom died when I was young. Before middle school. It was awful, but we survived it, my sister and me. I got her through, I helped take care of her, and having her there to take care of helped me, if that makes sense. She was—she is—the best person in the world. It was like we shared a brain. When I was in high school, she died. She was at a party on the beach and it was late at night. I wasn't there and none of her stupid, drunk friends noticed that she was gone. I woke up the next morning and she wasn't in her bed. The last thing anyone heard her say was that she was going swimming."

Gabrielle put a hand to her mouth. "Alison," she said. "I'm so—"

"No. Please. Just let me talk. I've never said this out loud before. My sister died. She walked alone into the water, and nobody stopped her. It was the worst, most horrible thing that ever—except..."

I wasn't sure how to say this part. "Except. When I moved to New York, she came back. And I don't know exactly how it works, but she was a fish. She is a fish. My sister is a fish and she lives in a pickle jar. The jar I brought on the plane with me. You just can't see her. I don't think anyone can. Nobody can, nobody but me.

"I was so happy at first when she came back. I took her everywhere. It was like she was haunting me and I thought it was the best thing that had ever happened." I took a deep breath. "But after a while, she started to fade. She's sick, I think. She doesn't want to be a ghost. I know this sounds crazy, but she needs to move on, she needs me to let her go, and she needs the ocean for that to happen. And I think she knew somehow you would help me find an ocean. She knew you would help us. And she was right, and it's been kind of perfect, being here with you, except the jar, except now you're going to think I am out of my mind." Gabrielle uncrossed her arms, fiddled with the silver watch on her right wrist.

"And it's okay if you do. It's okay if you want me to leave and never speak to you again. I would understand. I know I sound crazy. I don't know if I would believe me either."

Gabrielle looked at me for a moment. It was darker now, in the alley, and her eyes shone.

"When?" she asked.

"When what?"

"When would your sister like to go?"

I felt salt water burn at the corners of my eyes.

"Tomorrow would be nice," I said. "Somewhere quiet."

She nodded. "Tomorrow. Of course."

The sun had finished its descent and we had been thrown into pitch-black, perfect darkness. I could only see the outline of Gabrielle, who believed me, who believed in my sister.

"Thank you," I whispered. Her figure leaned forward and kissed me on the forehead like a priest bestowing a sacrament. We were standing so close that the backs of my hands brushed against hers. I didn't move. We stood there in the heavy Florida air. We stood there and we didn't speak and we let the night come and quiet the world around us, let the stars rise and reflect like shards of glass in the blue-black water, where fish swam deep and boats glided home and waves crested, then crashed onto the shore. Everything going home. For a moment, it was a perfect world in which everything was home.

Unbelievably, after revealing my deepest, darkest secret to Gabrielle, I found myself following her to a place called the Conch Shack, a restaurant on Duval Street in a stretch of stores that would have looked like a strip mall if they hadn't been in downtown Key West. *Restaurant* wasn't quite the correct word—it was an open window in a blue-painted wall wedged between two shops selling novelty T-shirts and postcards with pyramids of shot glasses and racks of bathing-suit cover-ups in the front windows.

There was a line stretching down the block, and we stood on it, and we waited quietly, both of us keeping our thoughts to ourselves. Or maybe we were out of thoughts. What else was there to say? My body was loose and light, like it might float a few inches off the sidewalk.

When we got to the front of the line, Gabrielle said, "Hey, Joe."

"Gabrielle!" a guy with a sandy mop of hair said. "I hardly recognized you!"

"This is Tara's son, Joe," Gabrielle said to me. "Joe, this is my friend from New York, Alison. We work together." Key West was turning out to be a very small town.

"Nice to meet you, darling," he said. *Darling*, Joe's version, had eight *a*'s and no *g: daaaaaaaarlin'*. I hadn't realized how much I missed the immediate familiarity that was a characteristic of life in the South. I was *darling, daaaaaarlin'*.

"Your mom is amazing," I said. Joe smiled like this was something he heard quite often.

"She's pretty magic," he said.

We chatted for a few minutes. Joe was learning how to be an underwater welder. My sister was a ghost fish and this blond boy would one day work in the ocean. I was starting to realize that if you squinted your eyes, maybe every tall tale and mythical creature existed somehow in the big, complicated world.

Gabrielle ordered fried conch for us, which I hadn't tried before. Around the back of the restaurant, there were sticky picnic tables in an empty parking lot with faded white lines. We sat at the only empty table and Gabrielle unpacked the brown bag, oil from the fryer already seeping through. Conch and fries and white paper napkins, plastic forks, and two Heinekens in bright green bottles.

"Sometimes I wish we worked in a restaurant like this," I said.

"You don't mean that," Gabrielle said, sliding one of the cardboard containers of fried conch toward me, fingers already greasy. "This isn't even really a restaurant, it's like a fast-food window."

"But it's simple. There's no reservations and no pressure from Chef or needy hotel guests. There's no city," I said as I picked up a piece of conch. It was hot, too hot, and it burned the tips of my fingers. I put it back down in the red and white cardboard container it had come in and rubbed the grease from my hands onto a paper napkin.

"No city?" Gabrielle asked. "Are you tired of New York already?"

"Yes?" I answered. "Maybe? I don't know. I mean, my sublet goes until next summer so I can't leave until then. But it's December, and look at us." We both had pink noses and brown shoulders from the sun; we were eating juicy pieces of fried conch and wearing denim shorts and sleeveless tops. There was not a single puffer jacket in sight. It felt like a failure that I'd lived in New York for half a year and I could already imagine leaving. I slumped a little at the thought, and Gabrielle noticed.

"Once it's spring and warm and everyone gets all feverish with it, there's nowhere better than New York," she said.

I looked at the table. Someone had carved AC WUZ HERE in the wood. Everyone wanted to live in New York, didn't they? I felt like I was just learning how to form my own opinion about things. The air was hot and heavy. I didn't want to live in a gray city, I wanted to live in the sun where I could breathe.

"What was she like?" Gabrielle asked. "Your sister."

It had been so long since anyone had asked me about her. It felt good to talk about her—her shock of blond hair, her skin that flushed pink and stung after more than three seconds in the sunlight, how she could be both rebellious and serious, how loyal she was even when she was young, how she was the funniest person I knew. Had known? Tenses were tricky. Insects chirped from the edge of the parking lot and I realized it was late.

"You two were close," Gabrielle said.

I wondered if she actually believed me, believed that my

sister was a fish, or if she thought I was acting out some kind of trauma or grief and she was going along with it. It would definitely be a good story for her—invite a friend on vacation who turns out to be absolutely nuts, who believes her dead sister lives in a jar. Batshit. Certifiable. Hilarious, right?

I felt angry just at the possibility, but then I imagined how it could have gone. In that dark little alley, I'd expected laughter or doubt, at best, and at worst, her accusing me of being crazy and kicking me out with nowhere to go in this candy-colored town surrounded by the sea. Did it matter whether she pitied or believed me? I decided that it didn't. I chose to believe in her kindness the way she believed in my ghost.

"Yes," I replied. "We were really close. Thick as thieves," I said, echoing a sentiment my grandmother used constantly when we were young. "Do you have a sister?" I asked.

"Nope. One younger brother. He's a sophomore in high school at the same boarding school I went to, in Virginia. He's pretty much grown up there, so we aren't close, but I think that being there is probably better than being around my parents."

"Do you see him much?"

"I visit him at school a couple of times a year. He avoids family holidays too. His best friend from school, Jack, has a big family in Atlanta, so he usually goes there for holidays and school breaks. They're Jewish, so I guess my brother celebrates Hanukkah now." Gabrielle laughed a short, sarcastic laugh.

"It used to infuriate me, how my parents couldn't get their shit together, couldn't be decent people, but when you've been disappointed so many times, you sort of…grow a callus around your hope."

"That is both disgusting and poetic," I said. She laughed for real this time.

"I'm exhausted," she said. We were the last ones sitting in the empty parking lot behind the Conch Shack. I was tired too and anxious to get home. It was my last night with my sister, after all, if things went according to her plan. I wanted to say *Good night, love you, sweet dreams,* one more time. I felt hollow, and the hollowness was sad in the warm salt air. We gathered up the trash we had spread across our table, threw it in one of the metal cans at the fringe of the parking lot, and walked home.

I could see my sister's pickle jar on the windowsill when I opened the bedroom door. The light from the lamp on the dresser made the water look almost clear. The cloudiness was gone.

"Hi!" I said as I walked past the window to the bathroom. I didn't have to whisper now that Gabrielle knew. I turned the water on to wash my face, talking loudly over the sound so my sister could hear me in the next room. "I told Gabrielle about you. I'm sorry I waited so long. She believed me. She believed in you."

I dried my face on a fluffy washcloth that Tara had left in my bathroom before I even knew she was Tara, before I even knew that a world existed in which I could tell Gabrielle anything, everything.

"I understand now," I said. "I understand needing to go, to have space, not to be stuck." I swallowed the lump in my throat. "I'll miss you. I will miss you so much. But I understand. You have to go."

I poked my head out of the bathroom. I hoped she was doing a happy zip around her jar, but something was different. The jar was on the windowsill. The water in the jar was sharp and clear. It took me a moment to understand what I was seeing: The glass jar was empty. My sister was gone.

The room narrowed to a pinpoint. I put a hand to my mouth as all of the air in my body disappeared. My sister was gone. There was so much I'd wanted to ask her still. There was so much I'd wanted to say, like *I'm sorry, I'm sorry, I love you.* I picked up the jar, walked to Gabrielle's room, and knocked. I watched my closed fist rap on the white wood as if it were attached to someone else's arm. Gabrielle opened the door. Her face looked long and tired. "What's wrong?" she asked. I held up the jar.

"Can you see this?" I asked.

"Yes?" she said. "Your jar of water?"

I nodded. I felt my face crumple, like a wadded-up gum wrapper. "And it's just water? You don't see anything else?"

"It's an empty jar. Wait. Is it—?"

"She's gone," I said. "She's not there." My legs felt wobbly, as if they were about to stop working, and I sat on the floor in the doorway of Gabrielle's room. I knew, just like I'd known it was her the first time I saw her, that it was over. She was gone. She hadn't needed a perfect ocean or an elaborate plan; she'd only needed me to be okay, to let go. She wasn't haunting me because *she* had been stuck on something all these years; she was haunting me because I had been. I said this out loud to Gabrielle and she knelt on the floor beside me, a hand on my back, like I was very young or very ill.

"She needed to go," I said. "But I didn't get to say goodbye."

Gabrielle stood up quickly. "Tara will know what to do. I'm going to call Tara."

Gabrielle's belief was moving, but I knew my sister was gone. Her absence was sharp, like a knife slipping between my ribs. But she was better now, free from the purgatory of a glass jar and a voiceless body. It was better like this. I could believe that. I started to say that to Gabrielle, but she was already pacing around her room on her phone, listening to the other line ringing.

"Tara, hi, it's Gabi." I hadn't heard her refer to herself as Gabi before.

"So sorry to call so late—oh, right, of course. Could you come over? It's a bit urgent. Yes, everything is okay, we just need your help with something. Okay. Okay, thanks, I'll unlock the gate.

"She's coming," she said. "She was just walking out of bingo. She won the jackpot. One hundred dollars." Gabrielle smiled but her lips looked thin and pale. "She's taking Nancy home and coming straight here."

"You really believed me," I said.

"Of course I do," Gabrielle said. "Of course."

⚬⟊⟋⚬

Tara came through the back door. She paused for a moment, hands on her knees, almost wheezing. It seemed impossible that she was still wearing the same green T-shirt and denim shorts. It didn't seem like it could still be the same day, that twenty-four hours could contain all of this.

"What happened?" Tara asked, short of breath.

I stood up, holding the jar with both hands. I walked into the kitchen and set it down gently, so gently, as if it were a cracked egg, on the island.

"You made me run over here for an empty pickle jar?" Tara asked.

Gabrielle and I looked at each other.

"It was a fish," Gabrielle said. "It was her sister."

Tara walked to the jar, picked it up, held it gently in her two hands.

"I'm so sorry," she said, looking at me with her bright blue eyes. "I'm so, so sorry." She pulled me into a hug and squeezed me so tight, it almost hurt. It was comforting to be hugged like that, like someone loved. She put the jar back down in the middle of the island.

"I think we all need something to eat," Tara said. "My mama always said to feed a death, starve a birth."

"Isn't it feed a cold, starve a fever?" I asked.

Tara rolled her eyes. "That's an old wives' tale."

She never stopped talking, cheerful but frank, as she turned on the oven, took things out of the fridge and put them back in. She was a chorus of drawers opening and shutting. Gabrielle and I sat on bar stools next to each other. I picked at the cuticles around my fingernails. Gabrielle stared sadly at the jar.

"I think we should still let her go. In the ocean. Like she asked," Gabrielle said.

"Another funeral," I said. I couldn't stand the thought of letting my sister go again, but Gabrielle was right. My sister would have wanted something ceremonial. I wondered if she had known, somehow, that Gabrielle would know exactly what to do and say, and again sadness rose heavy in my throat.

"Y'all can borrow my boat. A real Viking funeral. Except don't set anything on fire," Tara said.

"You have a boat?" Gabrielle asked.

"Yep. Your dad pays very well. Cacio e pepe sound good to you gals?" she asked.

It was almost impossible to feel morose with Tara bustling around the kitchen, moving like a tropical storm from cabinet to pantry to stove. She cooked a cauldron of pasta, forced us each to take a few bites, then put the rest in the fridge and poured us all enormous goblets of wine. We drank those. As she cooked and poured and cleaned, Tara asked me about my sister, my fish.

"Tell me everything," she said. "Every little thing."

So I told her about my sister's obsession with sea glass and the night she appeared in New York, floating outside of my apartment. I told her about my sister's ability to French-braid better than anyone else I knew and that she was not a fan of Noah from the start ("I think I would have liked your sister," Gabrielle said). I told her I'd always wondered if my mom and my sister were up there, or wherever the whatever-after was, keeping each other safe.

When I ran out of things to say about her, Tara regaled us with When I Was Your Age stories. Her life as she described it was a combination of a glamorous musical and an epic odyssey: adventurous and splashy and a little unreal. Florida was growing on me. It felt slightly separate from reality, surreal in twisty, magical ways. It felt like home, like Awnor, but with the hard edges sanded off. We laughed so hard we cried, which was better than just crying.

Eventually, Gabrielle glanced at the clock on the oven and said, "Oh my god, it's five in the morning. The sun is going to come up soon."

"Oh Lord. Y'all let me go on like that too long," Tara said.

She grabbed the dish towel that was tossed over her shoulder and hung it on a fish-shaped metal hook above the sink. I wondered if I would ever be able to see a fish again without thinking of my sister. I hoped not.

"I'm going home to get some shut-eye. Call me if you want to borrow the boat—it's in the water at the city ramp on Eleventh Street. Joe can drive you too."

"Thanks for everything, Tara," I said. Gabrielle hugged her and Tara blew kisses as she walked out the door.

"She's your fairy godmother," I said.

Gabrielle nodded. We were bleary-eyed, and I was suddenly so tired, I felt like I was made of wet concrete. I was too shocked and raw to be sad yet but I could feel it coming, an itch in the back of my throat.

"I need to sleep a little too, I think," I said.

Gabrielle yawned in agreement. "What do you think about going out on the boat?" she asked.

"I like that idea," I said, after thinking for a moment of my sister in her jar, waving her fins. My sister in real life, sitting next to me in the sand after school so many years ago. "I think she would have liked it that way, to be let go deep in the ocean."

Gabrielle nodded. "Whatever you need," she said. "I'm setting an alarm for a few hours; let's sleep, then tell Tara we want the boat. Does that sound okay?"

I nodded. She wrapped an arm around my shoulders, squeezed me, then slid off the bar stool.

"Night," she said. "Love you, Alison."

I sat in the kitchen by myself for a minute. I traced the label of the pickle jar with a finger. The sticker was starting to unpeel from the glass. It was the luckiest jar in the world, to have held my sister for so long. I went to my bedroom, pulled all the blinds shut, and got in bed.

I woke to Gabrielle shaking my foot. She put a cup of coffee that was still steaming on my bedside table.

"Tara said Joe can take us on the boat, but he has to work tonight, so we need to meet him at the boat ramp soon. Are you okay with that? It's noon now."

"Okay," I said with a yawn. "I'm getting up."

"Do you want to say something?" Gabrielle asked. Her eyes were dark with worry or care. "Do you want me to say something?" she asked.

"Maybe," I said. "Thank you." I rolled over and closed my eyes. I listened to Gabrielle walk to the door and pause for a moment. She whispered something that sounded like *I love you*, and then left. I lay facedown for a moment, so overwhelmed by my sister's absence, Gabrielle's belief, that I felt flattened. I got up and showered, rinsing the layers and layers of the night before from my body: sweat from walking around Mallory Square, the greasy smell of the Conch Shack. The blue feeling was harder to wash off, impossible. It wasn't the sharp point of terror and anger and sadness I'd felt after my sister—the one with the human body and the blond hair that turned white in the summer sun—had disappeared into the waves. It was duller; it was an ache that throbbed, like a bruise taking forever to heal. But there was also a little glimmer of relief, the light under the door of a pitch-black room. I was no longer haunted. My little sister was gone, but hadn't she been gone for years? She was no longer trapped inside a glass jar, witnessing a world she couldn't fully participate in. I was ghost-less. I was alone, and it was lonely, and it was also a freedom I had never experienced in my whole life. My sister was okay. She wanted to go, and so she had gone. In a way, I was proud of her.

I toweled off and dressed in my black bathing suit. A funeral suit, I thought. My sister would appreciate the irony of that. I pulled cutoff shorts and a T-shirt on over it. Gabrielle had gone to the grocery store and returned with a jumbo-size tub of Skippy peanut butter, a loaf of bread, and a bottle of expensive-looking champagne. She'd made eight peanut butter sandwiches for us to take on the boat and put the champagne in a cooler on ice. It occurred to me that Gabrielle would be a good mom someday. I wrapped my sister's jar in a yellow gingham dish towel and nestled it into the picnic basket Gabrielle had packed our sandwiches into. We loaded it all in the Jeep and she started the car. It was my fourth funeral: mother, sister, grandmother, fish. It seemed like too many funerals for twenty-three years.

Gabrielle parked in the lot filled with pickup trucks attached to the empty skeletons of boat trailers. To my happy surprise, Tara was there, wearing all black, from her baseball hat to her Crocs. I was glad she had come. Joe was shirtless and shoeless, sitting in the boat.

Tara said hello as we climbed in, but even she was subdued. Everyone was quiet, respectful, but the mournful tone the day was taking on didn't feel quite right. I was trying to figure out how to fix it when I heard the hiss of a beer being uncapped.

"Joseph Taylor, don't you dare," Tara said. "You're driving."

"It's just one, Ma," Joe said a little defensively. *Ma* had a *w* on the end, *Maw*, a long hug of endearment. "Besides, you can drive the boat too."

Tara took the beer from Joe's hand and downed it in one gulp. Her neck was elongated as her chin tipped upward to catch the waterfall of Budweiser. It was somehow an elegant sight. I caught Gabrielle's eye and we both started laughing. Tara finished the beer, wiped the corners of her mouth, and tossed the bottle in her green plaid beach bag. Joe rolled his eyes and started the engine.

I don't know names and types of boats but this one was big and fast and painted red. There were padded seats in the front and the back. I sat in the front and Gabrielle and Tara sat together at the back, behind Joe, attempting to talk over the roar of the boat's motor and the chop of the ocean beneath us. The boat skipped over the water like a smooth stone on a still lake. It was a ridiculously beautiful day. The ocean and the sky were almost identical shades of bright, bottomless blue. After a while, Joe slowed the boat and pointed to a glimmer in the distance.

"Dolphins," he said in his Florida drawl, and he was right: A family of dolphins were surfacing, their bottlenoses first, then the slant of their mouths, their slick gray skin. We were deep in the Gulf of Mexico and it was another world, a bright and watery planet. He steered the boat farther and farther into the ocean until the land behind us turned into a speck, until it was nothing but sea and sky. If I believed in heaven, that day was what it would look like: Blue, blue, blue. Blue as far as the eye could see. Farther, even.

"How's this?" Joe asked.

I hadn't asked if he knew what we were there for. I didn't know if he understood or believed in what was happening or if he even cared, but I was glad that he was there, at my sister's funeral. We'd been alone together for so long. It would have made her happy to be surrounded by people who believed in sunshine and the ocean and love and her.

"Here is good," I said with a nod, feigning confidence, like I knew how to do this the right way, knew what my dead sister who had been a girl, then a ghost in the shape of a fish, then, simply, gone, would have wanted. But I knew there wasn't a right way, just like I knew there wasn't a wrong one.

Joe walked to the back of the boat and tossed a small metal cross attached to a long chain into the water. For a split second, I thought it was some kind of religious token and then I realized it was the anchor.

Gabrielle carefully unwound the towel I had wrapped the pickle jar in and passed the jar to me. She and Tara joined me at the front of the boat. The lid was still green, the label barely clinging onto the glass. I cradled the jar in my hands and stood on the bow of the boat. It rocked gently beneath me, an almost imperceptible up and down. I couldn't believe how blue the water was. I wanted to bend my knees and jackknife into it.

"Do you want to say anything?" Gabrielle asked.

"Um," I started out, feeling tentative and a bit self-conscious. "I thought about reading a poem, but I could just see her rolling her eyes and saying, 'That's *your* thing, Al.' So instead I'm going to sing the song she would ask our mom to sing to her every night. I thought it was such a weird song, but she loved it. It was creepy but there aren't many other songs about someone named Clementine. And when our mom wasn't there or wouldn't sing it, she would ask me. I never said no. She was a hard person to say no to. So I'm going to sing that song now."

I took a breath. First boat, first fish funeral, first time singing in public. I began, a little embarrassed, my voice wobbly.

> *In a cavern, in a canyon*
> *Excavating for a mine*
> *Dwelt a miner, forty-niner*
> *And his daughter, Clementine*

Tara joined in, her honeyed voice bolstering mine, and then Joe did too. Gabrielle didn't know the words but hummed along, and there we were, a chorus, singing for my sister.

> *Drove she ducklings to the water*
> *Every morning just at nine*
> *Hit her foot against a splinter*
> *Fell into the foaming brine*

Oh my darling, oh my darling, oh my darling, Clementine
Thou art lost and gone forever
Dreadful sorry, Clementine

Ruby lips above the water
Blowing bubbles soft and fine
But alas, I was no swimmer
So I lost my Clementine

After the last *Clementine*, I unscrewed the lid from the jar and slowly tipped the clear water out into the ocean. Something deep inside me swam toward the surface. *Thank you*, I could almost hear my sister say from across whatever sea of reality separated us. *I love you*, I sent back. When the water was gone, I screwed the cap back on the jar and carefully put it in the bag. I would keep that jar forever.

It wasn't what she'd planned, exactly, or maybe it was. I knew she would have loved it—the speedy boat, her sad song, even Joe, shirtless and suntanned.

"Amen," I heard Joe murmur behind me. I turned to face them. Tara and Gabrielle were both wiping their eyes. I felt that salt-sadness too, but I also felt light. She was gone, on to the next world, no longer tethered to a form she didn't belong in. I hoped she was free.

Gabrielle popped the bottle of champagne and we *cheers'*d to my sister, Clem, with pretend cups because, of course, we'd forgotten to bring any. We passed the bottle around, taking big glugs of the expensive champagne. Before long, Joe was cranking the anchor back into the boat and we were putting plastic baggies and the empty bottle in the picnic basket. I looked back only once to check and see if she was really gone. On the ride back, Gabrielle sat in the front of the boat, next to me. She held my hand the whole way home.

Impossibly, we still had three days left in Florida. When we got back from the boat ride, I crawled in my bed and slept until the next morning. It was a dreamless sleep, a coma. When I woke, I felt sadness like a dead tree felled across me. It was physical, the sadness, heavy in my chest and raw in the back of my throat. But finally, I felt like someone new, or closer to it. I was here, myself, and there was something else too, something that was me but that could also hold my hand and walk me home. I rolled over, closed my eyes, went back to sleep until the sun hung heavy in the relentless blue sky.

For the next couple of days, the rest of our "vacation," we went to the fancy hotel beach, lay in the sun, ate French fries and drank Diet Cokes, switched to beer when it was happy hour. Budweiser was growing on Gabrielle, which surprised and delighted us both. The days were tinged with a blueness that I could tell we both felt, but we still laughed, talked, swam, let the water dry on our bare arms and shoulders in the hot sun, let our skin feel taut and gritty. I'd forgotten how much I liked that feeling of salt and sweat drying on my skin, that feeling of being a little bit dirty, a little tangle-haired and wild.

One day on the drive home from the beach, Gabrielle pulled into the parking lot of a strip mall and stopped the car in front of a pawnshop. Outside was a yellow sign advertising golf clubs and watches.

"I have a surprise," she said, "if you're up for it."

"What?" I asked.

She twisted the key in the ignition, turning the Jeep off, and climbed out of the car. I followed her to a small storefront. BLUE LAGOON TATTOOS read the white letters stenciled on the glass door. A mermaid was painted beneath, her scales chipping off in the hot, humid air.

"Wait, really?" I asked.

"I've already paid for two tattoos. It's refundable if you don't want to, but I'll do it if you will," Gabrielle said.

"Okay," I said without hesitation, surprising myself.

Two hours later we walked out of the tattoo parlor, our upper arms bandaged in clear surgical tape that looked like Saran Wrap. Beneath it, on the backs of our left arms, right above our elbows, we had identical, simple line drawings of a fish.

"Thank you," I said.

On our last night in Key West, Tara came over and made a low-country boil for us: pinked shrimp, corn, and big hunks of sausage. Joe and a few of his friends stopped by to eat and swim in the pool, and even Nancy, Tara's bandmate, made an appearance. I felt like I could breathe here. In six days, I'd found more people to hug, to eat dinner with and pour glasses of wine for, than I had in the months I'd lived in New York.

After dinner, Tara stood in the kitchen rinsing dishes and putting them in the dishwasher while Gabrielle sat at the island and talked. I left them alone, walked through the clean glass doors into the yard like a ghost. I sat in one of the lounge chairs by the pool. The water was dark and I thought about Leo and Greta, who were probably still on the futon in our apartment watching old movies. I decided when I got back, I would ask them to go for coffee with me. I would tell them that I wanted to be friends. And that I was finished with living in the city. I had to go back there for now, to my job at the June and my small apartment, but I'd been chasing someone else's daydream and I didn't want it. I wanted sunshine and salt water. There were so many things I wasn't afraid of anymore.

I could hear Tara and Gabrielle laughing in the kitchen, the nicest sound in the world. I loved Gabrielle. I hoped I would tell her that before whatever magic I was feeling disappeared, before this strange, impossible week was jammed into the back closets of our memories. I closed my eyes and imagined us staying here, living in this big, weird house, getting beers with Joe on the weekend, our shoulders forever pink from the sun. I imagined her teaching me how to kayak, how to make frozen margaritas in the fancy blender in the kitchen. I opened my eyes as a clear peal of laughter rang through the night air. All I wanted was home, sun, water, to live like a lizard in a warm cave, but I knew Gabrielle would flee at any hint of domesticity. I knew she would never leave the city she loved. But did it make me broken or did it make me invincible that I wasn't afraid of that, that I wanted her forever but knew I could reckon with that loss? Maybe that was why my sister had come back: to remind me of how I survived.

There were lights under the pool's surface that made the water look dark purple, an almost violent shade. I imagined peeling my clothes off, letting the cool water lick at every inch of my naked skin. I smiled at the dark warm air; I smiled at nothing. I wasn't that person yet, but maybe one day. I stood up and walked back inside and it was like I hadn't ever left.

We were waiting in line for security, and I was almost excited to go back to the city. Now that I knew it wasn't forever, I was looking forward to being back in the chaos of it, back in the restaurant and at Grace's after late-night shifts with Mike and Juan and Samuel and Gabrielle.

The plane's door was still open on the tarmac at the airport in Key West, Gabrielle and I were already buckled into our seats. Her bag was on her lap and she was rummaging around, looking for the pack of watermelon gum she'd bought before we boarded. A tube of lip stain fell out of her bag and rolled onto the floor. The sticker on the side said CHERRY-O. I picked it up and dropped the tube back into her bag.

"Thanks," she said, handing me a piece of gum before I asked. Such ordinary precious movements. I leaned back in my seat and looked out the window to the bright tarmac.

"Can I ask you something?" Gabrielle said.

"Sure." I turned to face her and the sun through the plane's tiny window lit up her face. Her skin shone like gold.

"You aren't going to stay, are you?" she asked. "I mean in New York." I thought again about the blue sea, warm sand, our shoulders pinking in the Florida sun.

"No. I'm not."

Gabrielle smiled. "I always wanted to be the kind of person who went on vacation and never came back," she said, closing her eyes, and a firefly of hope flickered in me, on and off, on and off.

The flight attendants walked down the aisles, making sure our seat belts were buckled and tray tables stowed away, and then the lights dimmed. I imagined the two of us standing up, sprinting off the plane, across the tarmac, and down the highway back toward the sea. I could see us living in that big house forever, spending our days in the water beneath the sun. But we weren't woodland fairies or mermaids; we needed jobs and other people and health insurance. But then again, my sister had been a girl, and then she'd been a ghost swimming in a jar. Nothing was impossible.

For a little while, I knew, we would go back to our normal lives in New York: working at the June and drinking too much on weekdays and avoiding Jen when we passed her in the park and going for coffee at Black Dog. But there was something else out here, something I wanted, something that didn't feel too far away from my fingertips. I was still grasping at air; I was alone in the world but no longer so painfully lonely, and I could sense the something more–ness just ahead of me.

The airplane started making a mechanical whir, and soon we were in the air, the blue of the Gulf winking below. Gabrielle was already asleep, her head resting on my shoulder. As the ocean got smaller and smaller, I leaned toward the window carefully, not wanting to wake her up. I put my lips against the plastic. There was nothing but blue beneath us, a blue shaped like my sister, whom I loved like I would never love anything else, who had reached out her hand and beckoned me forward.

"Goodbye, Clementine," I whispered to the ocean below. My throat was hot and tight. Tears rolled down my chin, landing in Gabrielle's hair without waking her up. I let myself cry a little as the ocean disappeared and we were enveloped in wisps of clouds. I didn't think she would mind.

ACKNOWLEDGMENTS

Ushering a book into the world is an art form of its own. Thank you to the many people at Little, Brown who made this book what it is, especially Morgan Wu, an incomparably kind and thoughtful editor. A huge thank you to Christopher Combemale, dream agent, without whom this book would still be languishing in my Google Docs.

Thank you, thank you, thank you to my mom, Margaret Barnes Pennebaker. The best part of me is the daughter of this brave and beautiful person, who taught me how to dream big dreams. And thanks to the rest of my home team: Cissy, Ned, Caroline, Lawson.

I would not have written this book without the generosity of the folks at the New School. Thank you so much to Lori Lynn Turner, Sidik Fofana, Marie Helene Bertino, and all my brilliant classmates and professors, who asked me questions I wasn't brave or smart enough to ask myself. Go, Narwhals.

Thank you also to the folks at the Virginia Center for the Creative Arts for the time and space.

Endless love and thank-yous to my New York family: Mills, Christian, and Gen—how lucky to feel like this place has become home. To my brilliant writer friends, thank you for taking my work seriously: Helena Grande, Daisy Cashin, Frances Rooney—what a gift to know you all and your words.

Thank you to the incredible (and incredibly fun) folks at Gotham Writers Workshop, especially Alex, Dana, Charlie, Emma, Sam, Street, Darren, Kelly, and Jen—it is such a joy to work with you all and our community of writers every day. And to all the booksellers and librarians who make the book world go round, especially Karen Anne Pagano at the Village Bookseller in South Carolina: There aren't enough words to explain how much bookstores and libraries have meant to me. Thank you.

The lines on page 124 are from Frank O'Hara's poem that begins "Light clarity avocado salad in the morning." My gratitude to the estate of Frank O'Hara for permission to use this excerpt.

And the biggest thank you to Davis Evans, who saw me through the everydays of writing this book. Thank you for making our life such a gorgeous place to live; for all the encouragement and Holiday Cocktail dates; for reading me a chapter of *As I Lay Dying* a few summers ago, which changed everything; for keeping us fed; for the music and coffee and walks; for always reading the earliest, messiest drafts. You're the best. I love you.

ABOUT THE AUTHOR

STUART PENNEBAKER is a writer and former bookseller from South Carolina. She now lives in the East Village, where she works and teaches at Gotham Writers Workshop. *Ghost Fish* is her first novel.